THE TENNESSEE HIGHWAY DEATH CHANT

Keegan Jennings Goodman

The Tennessee Highway Death Chant

KEEGAN JENNINGS GOODMAN

featherproof BOOKS

Published by
*f*eatherproo*f* books
Chicago, Illinois
www.featherproof.com

First edition
10 9 8 7 6 5 4 3 2 1

Library of Congress Control Number: 2015947375
ISBN 13: 978-0983186380

Edited by Tim Kinsella and Jason Sommer.
Cover illustration by Celeste Carballo and Cassandra Jenkins.
Design by Zach Dodson.
Proofread by Sam Axelrod.

Printed in Canada
Set in Hoefler Text

For Kitty, born to run.

The cosmos no god nor man did create, but it ever was and is and will be: an everliving fire, kindling in measures and in measures going out.

For souls it is death to become water, for water it is death to become earth; but from earth water is born, and from water soul.

Dead bodies are more fit to be cast out than dung.

—*Heraclitus*

One

ECCLESIA OF THE TRANS AM

Letter to the Editor, Monday, August 22, 1977

An editorial in last week's paper made a call to arms to dispel the local youth from the waters of the Hiwassee River. In response, I would like to venture the following remarks.

The article went great lengths to develop an image of the river as corruptor of youth. It is on the banks of the Hiwassee that our young people fornicate and frolic. The low-running brambles, rambling thickets, thorny underbrush, and tall swaying cattail hide our youth from the watchful eyes of the responsible adult world. Those passing along on the nearby highway cannot know that this river bank has become a spawning ground for miscreants. Last week's editorial was rather vocal about the sexual misdeeds occurring there, and we readers were, with adept writerly allusion, encouraged to imagine a number of colorful offenses: drinking, drug using, Satan worshipping, and so forth. Specific reference was made to cars equipped with enough horsepower and driven by kids with enough foolishness for both to reach ungodly speeds. There are indeed certain recognizable flourishes of the pen that belong to the hand of the righteously indignant, and last week's anonymous editorialist perfected such a flourish, turning a phrase that has stuck with me ever since: "Our Jordan," he wrote, "has become defiled by adolescent filth."

The force of this phrase, with its expert shift to metaphor, was nearly convincing on first glance. But then I wondered—which is the corrupting element? The youth or the river?

The author of the editorial seems to want it both ways. As I have said, he conjures an image of a river that has corrupted the youth, yet he reaches the heights of his powers of articulation when he lays the blame for the river's corruption upon the youth themselves. Perhaps the author imagines a process of mutual defilement by which the presence of one exacerbates the defilement of the other. Perhaps, though I do have my doubts.

We may also take as granted that the author of the editorial knows that the River Jordan has since Biblical times been and continues to be a filthy river. What the author is inclined to call filth, but I am inclined to call sediment, is common to both the Jordan of scripture and the Hiwassee of our valley and does not therefore constitute a meaningful point of contrast.

Why, then, was the comparison made? I believe the image of the River Jordan was invoked less for the quality of its water than for the quality—and convenience—of its metaphorical thrust, as well as for the hold it has over the good Christian imagination of the readership of this newspaper.

The River Jordan stakes its claim in the believer's mind as a solemn symbol of the promise of salvation. We see it at once as a vague token of liminal terrain and a fluvial avatar of hope. It marks the transition from this familiar world, wherein the soul is shackled to its bodily form, to a better world wherein the soul becomes joyously liberated from its material burden. It is inseparably connected with the notion of passing over and with the corresponding realization of the promised land. To cross the River Jordan is to cross from a life of toil to life eternal. To meditate on the meaning of the River Jordan is to meditate on the threshold nature of death, death as a transformative experience rather than as a terminus. This current, I believe, is responsible for the figurative weight of the River Jordan in our collective imagination.

The comparison, then, of "our own Jordan," the majestic Hiwassee, to the Biblical Jordan is not so ill-conceived. We have the advantage of being able to walk its banks and verify the coherence of the metaphor, playing witness to its figurative power as a watery threshold. Whatever sanctity to which it lays claim is not compromised by the sin that occurs upon its banks. No, that sin is the precondition for the cleansing force of the river. But before we call what happens down there sinful, let us pause and actually take a look to see with our own eyes that which some among us are so eager to condemn.

If we were to visit the riverbank, say, some late Friday night, we would encounter, first, a number of vehicles parked haphazardly just off the shoulder of the highway. There would be pickup trucks, sedans, and coupes passed down from parents to teens and therefore dented, bruised, and battered, but also cared for in a way first loves might care for the mementos that remain even when love has long faded. We would hear emanating from them the abrasive and insistent cadences of rock and roll music, and country tunes telling of unsavory characters running from the law, pursuing love and drinking away heartbreak. If we stop and take the scene in, we might catch the faint scent of marijuana smoke and will certainly smell whiskey in the night air. There will be peals of laughter, tough talk, voluble curses, easy promises—in short, the whole panoply of linguistic tools a youth calls upon in the grip of teenage excitement. If we listen closely, we might also hear splashing in the water, where two young lovers have decided to disrobe and go for a swim. Beyond the area illuminated by the headlights, we might find two kids embracing in the woods, or the noisy steps of a kid in the brush who, having had too much to drink, staggers off to find a place to relieve himself or vomit.

And insofar as this is true, it is all certainly objectionable. But there is a way to temper objection with a little understanding. The magnanimous listener hears more than the sententious gavel, and so, too, might we address this problem with something other than condemnation. We may, in fact, hear the conflicts, injustices, and minor triumphs of our own adult world translated into the language of youth. We might hear in these revelrous voices a more pristine likeness of our own verbal mishaps and indelicacies, distorted, as they are, by the complexities of work or home, but no more indicative of the need for love, pleasure, and beauty as our own. What is the chief difference between an insult adorning a young drunk girl's mouth and an insult hurled from wife to husband? In youth, a curse can strike us with the astonishment of an unexpected ornament; in adulthood, a curse strikes out at us with a venomous tongue. And what is the difference between a promise of love between two intoxicated eighteen-year-old kids and a vacant-eyed exchange of love repeated nightly, mechanically, between a husband and wife for years? The youth draws near with a promise, while the worn-out spousal couple uses that very same promise to shield themselves from the realization of the unbridgeable distances and irremissible terms of their mutual isolation.

In short, what we have before us, what has gathered at the river, is a demonstration of youth in all its rough and clumsy dismay. Our Hiwassee seems to me a site for the dramas of our adolescents to play themselves out as they will. The River Jordan is a threshold; through it we cross from corporeal life to heavenly life. So, too, is our Hiwassee a threshold; to cross it is, perhaps, to cross from youth into adulthood.

And why should we not expect these frolickers to get a little wet in the transition? Why wouldn't they get a little dirt on their pants and shirts, mud on their nightgowns, blood on their boots in the process of crossing such a fateful threshold? Why should we not expect that these adventurers will get lost every once in a while in the intoxicating revelries of whiskey or rock and roll? Perhaps they will drink into themselves a healthy fear of the Lord. Perhaps they will find their purpose in the arms of a woman, or in the lines of some heartsick country song.

Need I remind my readers that Naaman, that old Syrian leper, was instructed to bathe in the River Jordan seven—count them, seven—times? He had doubted from the start the power of those waters, and when he received his instructions from heaven, he started to walk away, as we are told by the chroniclers of kings, "in rage." He had expected the thrill and dazzle of the miraculous to be visited upon him, but instead all he was told to do was go take a bath. He went anyway, obediently, and when he dipped down into those waters he became clean, his skin as smooth as a baby's, his soul as joyous as one who had crossed over into promise.

We who are concerned for our youth would be wise to allow them the requisite time for making that trip across the Hiwassee, from the wilderness of callow childhood to the civilized regions of responsible adulthood, which, although fraught with hardship, will not be gained without the proper patience. It took Naaman seven dips down into those waters. We would have been remiss to have pulled him out after only six.

The next morning I woke before the rest of them and made my way through the thicket down to the bank of the river. The taste of last night's liquor was no longer in my mouth. There was no taste there at all, not of sleep, not of John, only thirst.

John says the difference between thirst and a dry mouth is something for heaven to sort out, and that when heaven comes searching for him, thirst will be the only thing it finds—no chassis, no engine—since thirst is not of the mouth but of the heart and of the night, and in the fervor of its human proportion. Thirst shares the quality of depth unique to the woods: a depth that cannot be stepped into. There it is before us, this thirst that will survive the body, and if it is glimpsed at the right time, under the right circumstances, at appropriate velocities, Jenny, then all horizons on the highway shall succumb to the single obscene opening of the can of beer, both mouth and eye, or the rapturous glass mouth of the whiskey bottle, because thirst, Evenene, may have its vile human dimension, but it also has its automotive contours and depths that can only be detected at the proper rotations per second.

And so I made my way along the path down to the river the next morning when I woke. The sky seemed to open up above the river, now liberated from the obstruction of the tall sycamore heavy with the foliage of late summer. But the murmur like that of living things remained. I knelt to the water, cupped my hands and brought them to my lips. I hadn't discerned whether my eyes had yet opened.

The next morning I woke early and slipped off to drink from the river. After swirling the water around in my mouth and swallowing it down, I backed away from the edge and sat in the cool grass. There was dew on the ground. The bottoms of my bare feet were wet with it. The dew was colder than the river water on my lips.

Thirst is somewhere deep in the body, according to John. When the body dies, thirst does not evanesce, but lives on. Having been shut up on the inside, but now liberated from the corporeal grip, the various thirsts that initiate motion in us move freely in the world, alighting on the souls of those it finds promising, so that some bodies, before they crawl to their final stop, learn how to kill thirst. John holds it self-evident that killing thirst is different than satisfying it. Satisfying thirst affirms motion and velocity, and these—motion and velocity—justify the presence of the body with its flimsy human machinery of blood, marrow, and piston. Killing thirst is self-effacement. It is daylight, John says, and cheap entertainment. It is the invitation to putrefy rather than crash, crumble, or fly away like some gospel song, there being no paved consolations against the current, against the swift decisions of a moving body of water, Jenny, knowledgeable of a single thanatomantic direction, a harrowing current to which we can acquiesce or curse, and both without bodily consequence, both in the utter stillness of the night's wide-open two-lane throat.

I leaned again down to the water's edge and drank from my cupped hands. The sun would be up soon and the great trunks of the trees here would be etched with its print. Already, birds sang. Their singing never coalesced into a single sound—it was always a disparate, voluminous multitude. If there was any taste in my mouth it was of sleep, and that taste was now receding into that fold of waking, drinking, waiting, driving, drinking, waiting, and of the firelight of the night before. I wiped my hands in the cool, wet grass. It was the next morning and I leaned back in the grass to listen to the murmur of the treetops. Maybe the breeze is, after all, this disembodied thirst John wants it to be.

When the sun came up the next morning it came up on all of us. I tried to think of it not as a miracle, nor as the brilliant lie that John says it must be, trying as it does to gain entry into the body, bringing with it the decompositional forces stored in the guts of the earth, as the consummation of human hands, as the enactment of rot and refuse, as the sedimented and swift convulsion of the will mouthed in the right direction, at the right speed. The sun, he says, reaches into the earth and lubricates the conceit that separates the highway from the voice it silences, the river from the expanse it feeds, the insect from the life it gnaws, the pretty girl from the silk she becomes beneath the perfect automotive caress.

He would say this to me when I returned up the worn path winding away from the bank of the river to where the rest of the kids would be sleeping, passed out on the tattered horse blankets, in the grass, in half-embrace, half-naked, still half-drunk. I would sit and watch him as he climbed out from underneath the quilt we shared, and clutch at the thought of the ascending sun as an everyday occurrence.

I tried to think of it instead as a sign that things could move forward. There are stories I know of people who have used the sun as a concrete tool to measure the progression of time. The idea is that time exists as some elusive aspect of motion, beyond the boundaries of the human mind, somewhere in the world, or maybe everywhere in the world at once. This scheme gives the earth direction: its journey can be measured by its relationship to the single fiery thought peeking above the horizon. I leaned back in the grass, shifted the weight of my body there, and stared at the moving water. I tried to think of the progression of time as a definite sensation, as a disturbance in the air, like the breeze. It was the next morning and had been for a long time. And it had been the next morning many times.

I wiped my hands dry on my thin white nightgown, backed away from the water and reclined in the grass. I closed my eyes and tried to feel the sun pass over me, the way it might move in stories over a landscape, or over the face of a lover or cop. When my eyes opened, everything was brighter. The riverweeds, in the sway of the breeze above and of the current below, tilted forward, and the light complicated the surface of the river as it pushed its own scintillating reflection back out into the world. And I remembered a story about an ancient and eternal mother who once harvested light itself from the surface of the water. She lived with her seven blind sons, and each morning she would walk down to the river near their home to gather water for the day's chores. On one particularly golden morning, as she was making her way through a thicket of reeds, she slipped and fell, and the old, cracked clay pot that she used was submerged in the marsh. As she groped for it underwater, she felt a vessel, suppler than her own clay pot, and brought it up out of the water. It was a basket, woven from the stalks of the rushes that grew in this part of the river. The basket shimmered in the light of dawn, and she decided she would try it out. She waded into the water and skimmed the open mouth of the basket over the surface. The water she collected gleamed gold with the brilliant print of the sun overhead. She stirred it, infused with sunlight, and it shimmered even more.

When she returned home, she looked again inside the woven basket and saw that the golden sheen of the water had remained. She set the basket down and called one of her blind sons to her. The young man approached and sat before her. She took the water in her cupped hands and splashed it onto his dull, unseeing eyes. He recoiled from its touch at first. But then images formed before him. He reached out with his hands as though to touch what he saw, and the world began to take on color and shape.

The remaining six blind sons were called over, and each recovered his sight by contact with the mysterious luminous substance in the basket woven from the reeds and rushes. The young men gazed around at one another, at first reluctant to make any definitive moves among the folds of this new vision, with its continuities of sound and sight and touch all linked now in the common living tissue we call the world.

Now that they could see, the house could not contain them, and so they went out into the world. They walked through the landscape, gazing at the beauty of mountain, hill, forest, and brook. They stood at the seaside and contemplated the horizon. They basked in the sunlight, and spent hours gazing at the rich configurations of the clouds. Each morning these seven brothers would wake and rush out of the house into the world, which had once been a place of darkness and a source of fear but was now a place of endless visual mystery. They returned exhausted each night, and each night the mother welcomed them in.

There is, I suppose, a certain way we have to learn to see further into things if we are going to keep seeing anything at all, and so it was with these seven brothers. Soon, they grew bored with the beauty of nature. They took to sitting in the fields, aimless, irritable, and unsatisfied.

One day, however, the eldest brother rose in frustration and wandered further than any of them had wandered before. He came to a village and was struck by the rich array of activity before him. He saw people talking, smiling, gesturing, all swept up in the current of a seemingly invisible but pervasive order. His feeling of bewilderment took on arresting proportions when he saw walk before him a young woman. Unable to look away, he followed her through the street and down a dirt path out of the village. His urge to look had changed into an urge to seize. And he did so, taking her in his embrace with the same voracity with which he had recently taken in the visible world.

Sometime later, he appeared before his brothers with the woman. Each in his own way was driven to seize her, and they did this plentifully and mercilessly. The image of the girl's body was for them a capstone to all the images of nature that they had been consuming, and they left the corpse there satisfied.

There is a picture of death to be seen in the ravaged body, and there is a picture of death to be seen in the hands that have ravaged. When the boys returned home, it was this latter picture of death that their mother saw; it was blood, and a certain inertia lingering in the hands. She perceived straightaway what her sons had done. And for several nights thereafter the men returned home with similar signs of gruesome acts, and that same mark of satiation lingering at the corners of their eyes. And it certainly was the eyes, she believed, that were the source of her sons' turn toward depravity.

She waited for the next moonless night. When it arrived, she crept down, the same woven basket in hand, to the riverside. It was a night of absolute darkness. She waded out into the water, which communed with that darkness, and once again skimmed the surface with the open mouth of the basket. The absence of light had with it an intensity that matched the previous golden brilliance. She carried the basket home, and waited for her sons to fall asleep.

She stood over them and sprinkled the black water onto their eyes. They woke to blindness, of course, waking from sleep into something even further still like sleep. They cried out for this lost thing: the visible world. The mother, brokenhearted for having torn the gift of sight away from them, told them that if they slept, they would see again. For once an image has etched itself into the mind, she explained, it remains forever, something like a visible echo that can be conjured with great clarity during sleep. And so the young men, longing to see the world again, were consoled. They closed their blind eyes and went to sleep.

It was not an easy path down to the river after I woke the next morning, but I had learned it well. There were smooth stones lodged in the ground. There were branches that stretched out from both sides, studded with thorns, that would catch on my nightgown as though the shoots were pulling me into dark communion with the forest itself.

The trees there were expressions of the river. They were the river doubled into rigid form, because their source of life was the water their roots gathered to shuttle nourishment up into the branches and leaves. The entire woods displayed this bondage to its source, like a secret that has escaped between the lips and flourished now into outright lies. At places in the path, the roots of these beings had broken through the parched ground and become exposed to the light of day. Dust from the trail and bird droppings had marred these roots. They bore the marks of cigarette burns and the scars from animals clinging to them, of bottles broken against them, of knives that had carved signs into them. I imagined the purity of their underground dwelling, and the purity of all buried things that have the strength to maintain their inner coherence and refuse the disintegrating fury with which the earth renews its own cyclical being.

The rain and the river itself were important parts of this cycle. Sometimes the path was muddy from recent rain, other times scorched hard in the sun. The weather here is what changes, and I have learned each step along the path in the midst of these changes. I have learned the steps but each morning is new. The scent of the river hangs in the air, and gets stronger as I wind down it. It ends where the woods breathe in from its own depths and opens up. In that opening is the river, gathering before the eyes, but pushing its way beyond their reach. The weather changes, but the river is always the same to look at, and it is always a new thing to see.

The river soothes, the river endures. The river rounds off the rough stone in its depths. Its age can be read in its glassy grain, but it cannot be fixed in place. The river falls, the river rises, the river renders each and every animal a fearful and watchful thing. It speaks, grumbles, gargles, hums, spills, swallows, vows and disavows, sneers, endures, and turns away. The maddening and vibrant song I sometimes hear it intone moves freely throughout the air. It is itself the cause of its own movement and so washes away the primacy of all other terranean substances. The fallen branch and the haphazard arrangement of rocks order the flow of the water and make that flow audible.

Nothing stands in the way, John sometimes says, of the human voice, no feature visible or invisible, high or low, nothing here on our side of the river to alter the dense jasper force of the voice, except the engine at night, or the consuming flames of the campfire at night, which wants our eyes more than our hearts, yet shall never have either. On our side of the river, Evenene, nothing ever alters the course of the human voice, whether slutty and sonorous, an end of the line you can touch the cream of, get its scent on the tips of your fingers, as the hand finds the waistline, Evenene, and dips down to pull up the honey of the first fateful turn of the biospheric key there, with spatial industry and temporal thorn, as the engines of the body jerk up the flash-hole and unholy make their way out, unholy down again.

Down and out, Jenny, he says. Down and out is the goddamn secret of this valley.

The process of decay is a promise made good, and it still clamors within us. It even has its own taste, a taste that I now tried to wash from my mouth as I bent my knees and leaned toward the water, taking it into my cupped hands, watching the rivulets run the course of my arm, downward, giving in to the urge to descend, and to the decay that furthers all descent beyond what the eyes can see.

I sat at the base of a sycamore and watched the water move by. A broad leaf of ivy was suspended from the bank. When I woke the next morning and sat before the river, I saw that the buoyant dance of this leaf of ivy was coupled to the churning movement of the water.

The river moves downstream in thought alone. The downstream gesture is not of lace like that of dancing, nor of tar like that of driving—it is geographic and abstract, a glimmer in the mapmaker's eye. But the water before me moved in all directions at once. It was doubled in the nettles and reeds that thronged the water's edge. A winged insect alighted on the broad leaf of ivy and beat its translucent wings, back and forth, against the invisible currents of the air. A gust of wind stirred the brambles, and the creature stayed firmly planted there, riding the currents of the air, tightening its grip, as the ground beneath him danced.

Insect life is eternal as motion is eternal, but beneath those two eternities, there was another force that had called the river into being. For it had struggled through the slick membrane of some vocal womb and had spilled itself here. It had made its bed here and this was the bed of the river, subfluvial, progenitive, and I knew that the troubled, varied churning of the watery surface, announcing all the turmoil inherent in speech, was a physical echo of the contours of the riverbed. It was a final bed and a first bed, granting life to the river, motion to the winged insect, and soft luminescence to the broad green leaf now padded with light in the early morning. They were harmonies to the stony submerged being of the bed of the Hiwassee River, and it transfixed me with a promise of perfect sleep.

There were other kids who inhabited this place with us. They were teenagers like us, and they had their own cars and trucks, their own booze and cigarettes, their own way of drinking as they sat facing the firelight. John called them his congregation.

They were up and moving about now the next morning when I returned to camp from the bank of the river. Some lay on the ground still, wrapped up in quilts that were soiled throughout and tattered at the edges, some sprawled out on horse blankets that had been storing in their fibers the dust and ash of the camp, sleeping bags that had merged with the ground itself. These kids were dressing now, yawning, stretching, blinking sleep from their eyes. Here was one walking off to relieve himself in the surrounding woods. The back of his thin white tee shirt clung to him with early morning sweat. His long black shoulder-length hair swayed back and forth as he paced through the camp. He stepped over a couple still enveloped in their blankets, and I listened to his boots tread upon the soft ground and watched him until he disappeared in the green brush.

There was one girl leaning against the hood of a pickup truck, one foot resting on the chrome bumper splashed with rust, smoking her morning cigarette, twirling her finger in the lace of the scarf she wore around her neck, her eyes downcast, shoulders slouched. And there was another guy, sitting upright, an open beer nestled between his crossed legs. He stretched his arms up over his head, closed his eyes, rotated his neck, then threw his head back and opened his eyes, as though to see the lingering effects of a long sleep in flight, expelled from the body and now drifting upward into the trees latticed above the camp.

Who were these kids – these congregants – scattered everywhere around the camp, looking about without seeing, pacing about without aim, sipping whatever beer had remained left over from the night before? There was another girl, cheeks rouged, applying lipstick, holding the gaze of her pasty face steady in a compact mirror. And yet another, long blond hair and freckles, kneeling beside her, fitting around her wrist an ornate brass bracelet, and yet another, looking east, then west, then nowhere, a beer in one hand, and with the other, pulling out stray hairs.

Who were these kids? I did not know. Their necks were dirty, teeth grimed, clothes torn, but I knew nothing about them—for they could not speak. They tried to speak, but the only thing that came out of their mouths was a garbled chaos of sound, consonant heavy, ugly and inexpressive, without inflection, without any familiar rhythm. Even when they occasionally tried to address one another, there was never that spark of recognition in the eyes or around the mouth of the listener, nothing to indicate the tacit passage of thought from one mind to another. They were deaf to one another's current of monotone, yet they acted together, congregating in dark concert with the inexplicability of this valley.

John says that maybe they dwell here as the dross of that cosmogonic fire in the great engine of being that dropped its transmission and stalled out long ago, or that they are the abandoned conspirators of a plot that slipped out of control upon a celestial highway and through the fingers of the demons that paved it, since the human body is a burden too heavy to bear the moment it crawls up out of the dirt to orient itself in a patch of sunlight or the alternating red and blue glow of an ambulance. I don't know.

The trees that surround our camp are gaunt but not barren. The breeze moves through them but still they say nothing. Their summer leaves stand in contradiction to their lifelessness. The heavy boughs of the sycamore, of the white oak and laurel—John knows all their names, says he learned them so he could curse them by name when drunk—exist for the sole purpose of complicating the shadows they cast out into the open glades. The tips of every leaf point to the ground as though they long for it, as though they are staring down their fate with cold resolve. But will they ever fall?

In stories I have heard, time grips everything and carries all along in a morgue of endless movement. The other kids here tell no stories. In the movements of their bodies, their incessant slouching, their insouciant gestures, their grim, stuttering mouths—there is only a mimicry of the abyss. When they are on their way to their drink, or already a longtime there, their eyes are always elsewhere, and when they collapse at night, their eyes are still opened to the dancing flame of the fire.

John says that there is a more excruciating law of flight implied in the form of the automobile, horror of the void more horrible because it can sometimes dodge or even outrun the scales that some call justice and others call blindness. The car has its own fire to animate its working parts. But here in camp, the flame takes a digestive form in the hunger that propels the maggot, worm, and mite toward that which the car has spurned.

When I woke the next morning, I went down to the riverside to wash the taste of booze from my mouth. Then I headed back up the path to camp and stood before the place where the fire had been the night before. Sometime over the course of the night, the fire must have gone out because the pit was cold ash, rimmed by charred logs. I held my hand over the ash, and moved it slowly, palms down, from side to side. There was no heat, not even the memory of heat, for the pit was cold, much colder than the surrounding morning air.

While crouching there, I saw a shadow appear and I looked up. It was one of the congregants, a burly young man with long curly hair. He knelt beside me and plunged both his hands into the ash, digging into the pit all the way up to his elbows. He then leaned forward and shoveled out the armload of ash and the spent embers, tossing it all to the side before plunging his arms down again. He placed his hand against the surface, paused, and scraped at it some more. He looked up at me. There was sweat on his brow, dripping down the side of his face. Then he took my hand and placed it at the bottom of the pit he had dug. It was smoldering. I could feel heat rising up against my palms in a strong and steady current. I pulled my hand away, and he dug further into the ash, scooping it away, setting it aside with care. Then he stopped. I saw there between his fingers a tiny flame emerge, licking its way up from beneath the surface. He made a clearing for it, giving it room to breathe, and it grew, then doubled, and grew more. He held both hands now over the flames, and continued to call forth the fire up from the ground. There was a pile of sticks someone had gathered, and he placed these on it, watching the thin trail of smoke rise up and vanish in the air.

I woke the next morning before all the others and walked the path down to the riverside. After drinking the water from my hands and sitting back in the grass, I opened my eyes and saw a man on the other side of the river.

He stood motionless before the rushing tumult of the Hiwassee. His rugged face seemed to have long ago exhausted whatever the river could do to it. Between us, the low-hanging branches whose leaves just brush the surface of the water seemed to inhale, then tense up, and give themselves up to the splintering force of the man's presence on the other side of the river.

I considered the dew on the ground, the light in my eyes, and the silence before me. The manifold wall of birdsong ceased. The wind rustling in the boughs of the trees above me ceased. Even the voice of the river, rising and rising, drifted from its body and coupled with the silence that had descended in the man's presence.

He was bearded, broad-shouldered, and thick around the neck. His body was broken but the messages it carried were not. He had come from some place else—some place where names clung to the body, incarnate and infallible, because now his figure effloresced into something readable: it was motionless and articulate and withstood the obscuring imprint of the sun, that bright lie, as John calls it.

I decided to call him Nathaniel.

I watched Nathaniel stir on the other side of the river. He plucked at the grass, scratched the back of his thick neck, threw stones into the water, lit a cigarette, scratched at his beard, gazed up at the leafy boughs overhanging the edge of his side of the river, shut his eyes, and stretched, arching his back and raising his arms. He did all these things in a shroud of serenity, but was doing nothing at all—not even waiting. If the human body is a finite series of movements, some slight and insignificant, others sweeping and momentous, and if these movements begin the day of birth and do not cease until the body moves no more but is moved through, then I was sure I could read him from my side of the river.

I heard once that the mist hanging over the river makes things more legible. The belief is that those inscrutable aspects of a human being are simplified and made to cohere when glimpsed through the nearly translucent veil of the water's imperceptible ascent at that moment just before it is caught up in the sky, transformed into mounting clouds, and sent back down in a torrent of innumerable drops of rain. It makes the human being into a word that can outweigh the need to speak.

This is nothing like what John says about the night. He says the night is what makes the world intelligible, and that only by virtue of a swift moving darkness can the flux of the material world be taken in by the mind, or the eye, or the mouth, depending on the hour, the speed, the thirst, or the sense of urgency clinging to the nerves.

The swift moving darkness blurs past the two of us when we speed down the highway in his Firebird each night, and it is this same swift moving darkness that contains mixed with it no deceit, no dull edges, no sunshining lie, no oppressive electricity, no cops, no future, no paramedic, no past, nothing to scare away the animals, nothing to complicate our streamlined rush down the highway, nothing to barricade love in all the most delirious and reproachful regions of the body.

But it was morning now as I watched this strange man from the other side of the river, and the night seemed to me an impossible distance. Nathaniel moved with labor through the thickets, closer to the water. He was shirtless, and he squinted in the sunlight. The frailty of his body was pronounced against the verdant green of the riverbank. He paced before the edge of the water. Then he retreated from it, stood back and tugged at his beard meditatively. No, he was not waiting for anything—he was where he belonged. He was in his own element, and that element was fierce and consigned to all impossibility: it was the void and abyss, and it had been fashioned from the twin terrors of distance and revocation.

I recognized the weak human flesh tone that tries neither to offend nor hide, and which, according to John, is an insult to the earth and the animals dwelling in the woods, is anguish and blight upon the river, in the valleys, upon the mountain, and distributed upon pavement. There was indeed something ugly about the surface of the man's vivid humanity there on the other side of the river, but I did not look away. His corporeal presence possessed a weight that seemed to anchor the entire world in which it moved. It reminded me of the birds that I could never see but whose songs I heard each morning by the riverside. How could something with such material substance not simply sink into the ground?

After I'd washed the sleep from my mouth the next morning, I reclined in the grass beside the river and listened. It is a lie to say the woods breathe. It is less of a lie to hear the river breathe.

John says a lot can happen on either side of vision, on either side of the earth, the palm of the hand, the moon, the silk of the throat.

The surface of the water appears as a swift plane of motion, ferrying the debris it catches from the world above, the thickly matted twigs of the cedar, pine needles, individual leaves that have detached themselves prematurely from the body of the trees that sprouted them to seize the sunlight and transform it into something solid. But beneath the surface, the steady flow of the current reproduces stability and equilibrium.

The same mystery is found within the flame. We do not know what happens there inside the flame itself. We do not know the origin of its need to move, and why this need is never sufficient to free the flame from the source of its burning debris. John says the fire wants to spread into the woods, wants to swallow the river, wants to consume trees, the mountains to the east of us, wants to return to the highway the logic it once had, a logic of direction and speed and perilous momentum. But the fire does not always comprehend its own will. It illuminates the vehicles parked at the edge of the camp, animating them with a force and nocturnal beauty that stands in contrast to their unidirectional habits on the road. They danced now, and that dance seethed like the frenzied flame as it tries to fly upward, to loosen itself from its substantial aspect of wood lying on the ground to which it is chained.

Talk, too, can do this, John says. It can dance with its shadow, and both dances are lascivious and crude and glimmer cheap on an overabundant surface, and the chrome or rusted grills of the faces of the cars joined in this dance at night, became expressive in the way they took on and shed new shadows. That is the place where physical memory lingers, and it spreads over other surfaces that constitute the minutiae of our lives here before the campfire each night.

At that time of night when the fire dies down, I feel even in my sleep the approach of the next morning and the hazy assurance of waking again. Even so, there is nothing to compel me to think of the night as the mere shadow of the day, because in those early, lost hours, the fire does not die out, but only retreats down through the layers of ash. There is no refuge of a final and decisive flame reflected in the pupils of those few others who remain awake sipping whiskey or beer, reflections that almost lose their composure as they increase in brightness and intensity the closer the actual fire gets to its last few gasps, bolting upward as it senses the approach and bitter fulfillment of its own extinguished promises.

The next morning I woke and I was the first to wake. John snored and uttered something venomous in an uneven tone in his sleep. He once said that he hates to breathe the same air everyone else breathes, and had been looking at the woods as he spoke, but now asleep he mumbled black verbal gusts of nonsense I could smell when too close. Even these were distinctively his; they bore the mark of having passed through him, holding his startled guts together just as deep shadows, it is said, hold together the insides of the woods.

He has said a hundred times that there's passing through, passing over, passing with, and passing on. But the transformative moment underneath the hood of the Firebird is not performed with the same success with which we make that transition from sleep to waking, from stasis to motion. That transformation is hidden from human eyes, eyes that have already been thrilled open by daylight, by the songs of birds and a dry mouth. The truth of such incremental shifts must remain unspoken and invested with the mysteries of the highway, must remain a ravaged word stillborn in the mouth of the world.

But it is different with the Firebird. Although no first-hand knowledge of the machinic transformations underhood is possible, the roaring eulogy of the engine appoints itself the voice that can speak the truth that remains unvoiced. It touches the sprawling night air and acquires the contours of the night itself. Which is always the last night, just as the new daylight is always the next morning.

John says that the rest of the damned county thinks that all beds must be taken lying down—the riverbed, bed of leaves, bed of lies, bed of pickup trucks. The morning can be taken in many different ways. Like the river itself, it holds with it innumerable corridors leading toward the same bed, the same mouth to empty itself of both bed and mouth, voice and passage, into those regions of the night where all becomes indistinct. The morning is a single clarion break, and the day the reverberation of that initial fracture out of sleep.

It is not a voice that comes to me because a voice can only be heard. Neither exterior, nor interior, neither terror nor consolation—the falling dictum of night signals the return of the familiar disjointed position of my body in this world, stretched out now, next to John, neither cold nor hot, but sheltering that immense mystery that can only survive for a few fleeting moments in the early morning silence.

The next morning, before the others had woken, I turned in the blanket to reach for John but he was not there. I got up and searched the place and found him standing near a pickup truck belonging to one of the young men who still lay asleep near the fire. I walked over, and John threw the door open. I slid over on the bench seat and he followed. We sat for a moment in the silence of the cab and gazed out the window at the dawning light.

Standing propped up against the odometer was a photograph, faded and curled at the edges. In this photo was framed the face of a young girl. Her lips were parted, in something not quite a smile, but more of a shy glow. John saw me looking at the photograph, plucked it up from its spot and handed it to me. She's pretty easy on the eyes, he said.

The camera had captured her freckles on her forehead and cheeks, and had unmasked her youth. Her large, blue eyes seemed to shine back a tease to the camera, maybe a challenge to its cycloptic mechanical eye. That challenge was the impossibility of capturing the life that suffused the girl's features, the force with which the machine had collapsed them into its two terrifying dimensions. There was nothing certain about her face there. It withheld from the camera what the machine seemed to want most, some definitive expression, something it could latch onto and incorporate into its immanent sense of space, arbitrary and utterly disposable. Through her slightly parted lips the front teeth showed, healthy and gleaming and possessing that secret collusion of animals with the brush, which evades the tendency of the eye to find, identify, locate, and name.

As I examined the picture, I realized that this girl was among us, that she was one of the congregants, and I conjured the image I knew of her from here in this valley. But that image was incommensurable with the one before me, though each beheld one and the same person. I looked away from the photograph and thought more about the girl as I knew her, a girl whose lips had endured the failures of speech, and recalled to my mind those few times I'd heard her muttering to another kid, in that form of speech that could never be speech.

Maybe this photo had been taken when she could speak, that it came from a different place, a different time, when the eyes, and her soft glowing backlit golden hair, the nose, the freckles, all those other parts of the face—the area between the mouth and the nose, the sweeping region where cheeks become chin, or the indeterminate terrain of forehead and temples—all those places on the human face that have no real names of their own—I understood that in everything taken as a whole, that somewhere there lay a sentience, detectable only by virtue of the capacity to speak, and that this had resolved itself into definite words, sentences, expressions, with these very features, and had been lain up somewhere in the whole of her visage.

John watched me from the driver seat where he sat. Then he stretched out his legs and plunged his hand into the front pocket of his jeans. He pulled out two coins—money that would always appear the next morning, whenever the need for it arose—and took the photo from me. He placed it face-up on the leather seat between us. He set first one coin, then the other upon the girl's beautiful eyes.

The sun is a bright lie. We contend with it less by day than by night, when we sit before the campfire drinking, listening to the woods beyond the firelight, thinking of the startled animals in the ditches on the roadside. Whatever we know about the sun has been taught to us by the fire.

They are said to be made out of the same thing and both forbid contact, one by its unbridgeable distance, the other by its interdiction to touch. What must link them is a third kind of fire, something that has to do with the eyes. If the blunted spot of light above us is a lie, then we are deceived nightly by its terrestrial appearance here among us, and have no explanation for this pit of flame we stare into while seated on our horse blankets.

What is deceitful about the campfire? John says the movement that breathes life into its flames is no movement at all. It strives for but never achieves the individuation of its parts. The flames lick one another, dance and scrape up against one another, ascend and descend, only to try to escape the material ground of their being, which lies in the dead wood itself.

By contrast, he says, the only true movement is that described by miles per hour, or rotations per minute, for that ratio does not depend on any heavenly being for its definition. Heat, after all, is both the cause and effect of fire. The flames desire to return to their source, which is not the human imagination but the sun itself, progenitor of all treacherous substances, for whom death is but an inward folding in on itself, death and life an emanation bluffing their way into the automotive heart, radiating outward rather than delimited by the controlled burst of the spark plug and the steadfast thirst of the fuel injector.

Sometimes, when we are all sitting drinking in silence, something stirs in John, and he begins to berate this horde of defeated faces, a single mass of beings which, like the fire, does not release its various moving parts, but lets them shudder against the four walls of night while chained to the brute fact of matter, domicile, and disease. Maybe the world will greet them the way it greets the river, with a silence that can never be affirmation nor denial.

I cannot understand how the animals can drink from that body of water. It is spurned each morning by our waking, and it is cursed each night by our sleep. We cleave to a curse, and this same curse gives the river its contours. John's words are often lost in that river. The force with which his voice surrounds its hearers, the grease with which it moves out of reach, the vague familiarity with which it urges us on—maybe the water is the only body capable of consuming that which flows from his mouth, in the same way the mouth of the Hiwassee River differs from the mouth that first named it: some human or divine mouth must have dropped the name into the water once, and the name, being of a certain weight, a certain extension, and a certain degree of motion, must have somehow remained submerged on the bottom.

Even though the other kids know nothing, we all somehow know this river, understand the shifts in color it undergoes throughout the course of the day. I am sure that we can all hear its logic in the country music our car radios pick up, can taste that same logic in the booze we sip throughout the day. We all somehow comprehend the coldblooded murmur of the water. We all perceive the presence of fish, of deadwood, of old fishing line, lost shoes, and colorful jigs. They are what is given the next morning, not new, not old, but presented for use, for ornament, for tease—I do not yet know. It appears, that's all, just as the money in the pocket appears each new morning, the matches that never run out, the gas in the Firebird, the empty highway leading down to the Gas-n-Go, the tavern, the garage over at Old Man Lory's place, where they all sit and drink and voicelessly make good on promises without origins, without destinations.

Even the setting of the sun—that bright lie becoming less bright and more captivating—is given in self-certainty. To ask how we got here would be like asking how the sun could crash with neither protest nor consequence into the horizon.

The other kids speak in a language I do not know, in a language that inevitably fails to ever sound like a vehicle to carry meaning.

They seldom make any sound at all. When they do, it comes out mangled, like an echo lost in the endless corridors of the soil, coiling around the roots of all living things.

Once, John said it was memory that was interfering with their attempts to speak, kicking up too much dust and ash for anything to come out right. Their eyes speak, though. They examine the distance, the fire, the river, the mountain to the east of us. But I do not know what they make of the mordant silence our valley here enforces upon them. It is an opaque place.

The next morning I woke and went down to the bank of the river. The body of the world was preparing for rain. The feeling reached into my own body, too, gripping my insides as I drank, down on my knees, from my cupped hands. Does the air thicken? Maybe—but in doing so it also thins out into nothing. That is the laughter and the last indistinguishable gasp, a curse to the lungs suspended between us here in the late August heat. It would be air that has ceased to surround that which rigidly stands against it, the solidity of the world, solidity of the word, just as sleep is nothing if not cessation of the voice, the thought, the step forward onto the dewy grass. The humid air crawls up through the spine the way thought has emerged over the course of millennia, so that our most recent ancestors had to stand upright to straighten and streamline the path it fought to forge to heaven.

And the feet surrender to the path. The body surrenders to the feet. But what surrenders to the body?

When I wake the next morning, he sometimes tells me not to stumble on my way, don't even breathe or think unless you're sure the sole of the foot has communicated to the head the confidence that yes we are on the right path, that yes we are river-bound, yes we are the perfected disavowals of all stillness and peace. Once, when I was kneeling on the bank of the river, my hands cupped to drink, he appeared there, the faded and tattered quilt wrapped around his shoulders, its lower fringes dragging in the mud. He knelt beside me, examined the sky with me for a moment and concluded that it might very well rain.

Even here rain scorns every part of the river, good and evil alike, by congregating in it, becoming itself rivered, by rivering consummate against its own impossible ascent, all bodies of flesh and water destined to tolerate the same sky. But it is not true that it rains on the righteous and unrighteous alike. There are depths of the river that never meet the atmosphere, sections of the water that are never inspired up into the air by the sunshine. All river water churns, but there must be, if only in the imagination or upon the soles of the feet, must be that one cupful or mouthful or handful of water that has never risen to the surface, but always remained underneath, having never been lapped up by deer, otter, or chicken hawk, never having even been gazed at by any eyes but fish eyes. The fate of water is to ascend, but that fate does not reach into every part of the body of the river: there we find water that has nothing to do with the ascent to the sky.

And water ascends as thoughts ascend in heavy shades of light that hover above the head, protect the head from heat or cold, from every bruising blow that threatens its collapse. He spoke of light leaking from the soles of his feet like trail-marking drops of blood, or from his head that verified the truth of what we all say but can never adequately utter. Thoughts shooting from the heads of thinkers, streams living in impudent ascent.

Yes, it might rain. When we arrived, it still might rain, and remained that way for a long time. I fell asleep with the sound of water moving into my dreams. John must've dreamed of water, too, because he was drunk by the time I walked the path back up to camp.

When I woke up the next morning after washing out my mouth in the river, I walked back up the dirt path and watched the other kids stirring in the camp. There were three girls on a quilt, its patches of white stained by the grass and mud. The girl in the middle lay stretched out on her back, her bare arms up over her head, glistening tan in the morning light. Her brown hair was fanned out on the quilt behind her. She bent her knees and crossed her legs, bobbing one foot in the air before her. The two girls beside her lay curled up, arms tucked in, heads buried in the folds of the quilt. Beyond these three girls, there was another girl, walking barefoot, brandishing a single red high heel shoe in her hand, gesturing to the boy who sat before her, legs crossed, his mouth hanging open, lips wet, slapping his keys against his jeans. And there were others—a blond girl wading through the tall grass at the outskirts of camp, and another, an unlit cigarette hanging from her lips as she rummaged through the heap of clothes beside her, and another kid, pulling over his head his sweat-stained tee shirt, and others, moving as I guessed animals might move if they had nowhere to go, nothing ahead of them but what had passed beneath the gray sky, stretching out with a subtlety and strength that could make iron and asphalt suddenly feel the need to answer to its dead, expansive silence.

It was the same progression to nowhere: the gas station, the Matinee, then the road, which had no before and no after, only night and a surface agreeable to headlights. There was a couple that had wandered off a bit to kiss in the bushes. There was the low murmur of the talk I cannot decode, which they form with great effort—unlike the effortless river of words from John's mouth—and nevertheless let fall to the ground, heavy in their tones, inexpressive of their anguish which can be read more clearly in the eyes than in the mouths of the congregants.

John appeared from out behind his car, zipping up his pants and yawning. He addressed the morning with a curse, some spit, and a loving gesture of the hands meant to express his deep appreciation, he once explained to me, of the crisis of unknowing and irresolution this place forces not only upon the body but upon the firm and gritty grip of tire upon the road, upon the empty head that youth loves but which the bitter world tries to fill with its tonnage of corruptible offal, grime which we innocent, babbling, knife-wielding babes should never have to soil ourselves with, Jenny, and which should not even be fed to the engine of the greatest, fastest, most tender-hearted beast ever to surrender itself to the feeble hands of humanity, yes, that is right, the Firebird Trans Am, which he caressed now in the morning overcast gray.

He went around the side of it to search the backseat for something to drink, or something to break, or something other than words to curse the woods with for having closed in on him over the course of the night, or the daylight for having turned the tables on him while he slept, or maybe the river for being the only voice other than his, and for swallowing up all the trash and drunken laughter that it had spewed out the day before. No river, he said, would compete with the pistons, with the engined ideas residing deep within its intelligent viscera of hoses, belts, fans, caps, pumps, its flesh that quivers for no one, responsive to the starter, its multitude nourished by grease and clearly defined edges, by the friendship of parts, neither interchangeable nor esoteric, a part that can be read by even the most dissipated eyes among us, he said moving through the camp, we're all subterranean, nothing to do but drink it down and follow the drink down, disentangle ourselves from the sunlight, from the bizarre longings of heaven, the lie of a journey that can effect no change whatsoever.

He was shouting now to his drowsy congregation. Is transformation of the body the means of salvation? Maybe for the animals this is true. Maybe for people eating insects and crushing earth beneath their bare feet it was true. Not for us. The automobile doesn't allow it. You place the car in time, throw it head-first into a unique flat plane of existence, pinstripe it black or red, charge a certain amount of interest per annum, brush the law with it in the predawn hours, and you'll get a second-rate satisfaction, the one you asked for, the one that keeps you from moving down an empty highway without acknowledging its emptiness, a satisfaction fit for the fool and his wise man, the junky and his paramedic, the cop and his criminal.

The automobile can never conform to this demand that materials be transformed over time, in space, in the black and white starry night, in the firelight, or the incessant thrum of the river. There's no such thing as a journey, no such thing as immensity, except that which sorts out the job of the hand, the mouth, the foot, the prick, he said. Life is not a gift received from a snake charmer. It is the poison stolen from the snake himself, vomited and translated into miles per hour.

The riverbed and a bed of blankets. A bed of coals and a bed of grass. The bed appears when you let your body fall to the ground, and that is all. It appears when one of you finds your youth beautiful, and it doubles, and you take each other in.

Here John paused, caught his breath and hit the hood of his Firebird. Let's go, he said, flower, petal, and whore to the floorboard. The kids began pulling up their sleeves, spitting, laughing, readying themselves for another burst of speed into the daylight. You are radiant and tough against this brilliant lie spiraling down through the tops of the trees, he announced to them all, you all make me want to get down on my knees and strike love eternal. They were all moving now, into their cars together, piling in, having been convinced once again, each time of the possibility or impossibility of movement, out of spite, obedience, or genuine enthusiasm—their faces were as impossible to read as their words. John, too, jumped into his car and started it up. He leaned across the console and pushed open the passenger-side door, and I slid in thirsty.

The next morning I pulled myself out from beneath the blanket we shared and walked down to the edge of the river. The sun was hidden behind the clouds. Everything was gray and my mouth was dry.

There was a story I heard once that said a fisherman was responsible for it all. This creator fisherman stood at the edge of a lake and gazed at the placid waters before him, idly casting his baits, lures, spinners, and jigs, and all the contents of his great divine tackle box. Yet the fish would not bite. He soon grew bored and lonely there on the bank.

Having exhausted his patience, he dropped his fishing pole, stripped off his waders, pants, and underclothing and entered the water. The fish saw him wandering around under the surface and grew afraid. Each step the fisherman took was followed by the ascent of a turbid cloud of sediment. The fish darted this way and that, using the murky water as cover. They hid in submerged logs, in thick weed beds, among clumps of mud and mounds of stone. All the fish trembled as they watched this creator fisherman walking among them. He couldn't see them directly, but he knew they were hiding.

He told them not to be afraid and asked them why they had not struck his bait. He attempted to ease their fear, saying that he was not hungry, just exceedingly bored, imploring them to join him, if even just to supply him with the pleasure of hearing another living creature's voice in friendly conversation. These underwater dwellers, however, did not believe him. They whispered among themselves that his worm couldn't fool us, so he's come down here with words to fool us, and they receded more deeply into their cover.

A great fury rose in the heart of the fisherman, and he began tearing at the deadfalls and weeds which provided the cautious fish with cover. When his destructive rage had run its course, he cursed the fish for their incredulousness one last time and left. He stormed up out of the water still clenching the sticks and mud and other debris of their underwater dwelling places.

Snorting and muttering to himself, he started arranging the sticks and mud, the weeds and stones into an upright form that we would now recognize as a human body, though it was lifeless of course, and neither moved, breathed, nor spoke. The creator fisherman stood face to face with the figure and tried to breathe into the mouth he'd fashioned out of algae, but the pebble eyes stared back at him lifeless. He offered it water but still nothing happened. He hit it, cursed at it, still nothing.

Finally, he stepped away from it and examined his surroundings. There beside him was his tackle box and his fishing pole with the line tangled in the reel. He saw the hook, and the bloated worm still writhing mechanically at the end of it. He unhinged the worm from the hook and placed it in the lifeless figure's mouth. It squirmed with more enthusiasm now, and the divine angler, with his two fingers, shoved the worm deeper into the mouth, and finally down the throat of stick and mud. The figure's pebble eyes blinked, his hand quaked and rose to massage the jaw, then to rub the eyes which could for the first time see out into the world. The tongue moved and the first words it uttered were words of gratitude. There was of course the sacred breath of life, the affective heart pumping blood, a certain amount of development, now dexterity of the joints, expression at the corners of its mouth.

The creator fisherman cleaned his man up, looked him over and was genuinely pleased. Before the two of them walked away into the sunset, the creator fisherman turned to the lake and shaking his fist in the air, shouted something obscene to the fish who had so cruelly refused his bait.

I woke the next morning and followed a narrow path upstream along the bank. The river narrowed too, and I saw Nathaniel on the other side striding before a pile of water-logged debris, evidently having been dragged up from the river, stacked without apparent order. It was a grassy open area. The sun cut shadows through the trees, and they were like stripes upon the natural contours of his body. In the strange array of refuse that had captured his attention, there was glass for sure, because I could see it glinting in the depths of the pile of trash. There were a few boards, muddied rope, the twisted claw of a deadfall, a rusted piece of hoop iron, the shredded remnants of a tire.

Nathaniel's hair was wet. The long strands in the back clung to his shoulders and leapt up into the air when he punctuated his words with feverish gestures. He was not only speaking to the waist-high brush pile before him—he was listening to it, too. He'd put his ear to the soft grassy ground, and then to the air, then to the brush pile. He kept a distance, but was compelled, too, by the force of his words to approach it and he did so cautiously. The open bottle of whiskey in his hand was an implement to indicate the momenta of pernicious unseen forces. It was a tool of fortitude.

It was not clear if he was speaking aloud. But there is a way of talking with the body that sometimes says more than the voice can. It was Nathaniel's movements, his stride before the pile of trash that evoked the image of a preacher. The texture of its incessant murmur claimed my attention for a moment, and I looked away from Nathaniel, down at the water itself.

At this narrow point of the river, the current picked up speed. The vocal character of the water doubled and I looked up again at him. His mouth moved, but its sound was swallowed up by the current rushing between us.

I have heard stories of stones pulled up from deep out of the ground, brushed off and swallowed for sustenance, stories of entire rows of timber taking revenge on lovers embracing after-hours beneath a stack of two-by-fours. It was therefore easy for me to hear him, or to take what I'd heard as words, moving along the currents of whatever thoughts he must have been directing toward that heap of debris. I tried to imagine what each discarded part would become if it did in fact accept the man's gestures, if it would in fact heed whatever pronouncement he had made about life, motion, and the ancient and universal purchase that can be gained with immolation, fire being the blood of the woods.

I could conjure no images that seemed to fit the prodigal assurance he must have wanted to imbue the trash with. This wood, panel, corrugated aluminum, tin, rebar—it all was what it had been and no more than that. Not even the sense of collapse and decay that creased his body when he leaned back to drink could make this debris into something new.

Strophic Choral Interlude: Haggard Analytics

We have all heard the rumor that Merle Haggard likes to get to bed at a decent hour. Let us for a moment follow him there and consider his body as it reclines, his eyes as they close, the back of his head as it falls upon the soft silken pillow, the lights out, as the song of crickets and other lowly creatures shuttle him into sleep. The sediment of the day's activities gathers before his mind's eye. Going from gunmetal black into buckshot round, then shaved down more slender and definitive, his thoughts now acquire a fine metallic shine that can move through the night the way fingers move upon the neck of a guitar. We see them there, ascending from the foot of his bed, mingling with the cool air coming through the open window, as the final moment of pictorial consciousness delivers our country singer into sleep—that most peaceful collaboration of dream and contentment upon the pillow.

Just as the eye must be allowed time to adjust to the dark, so, too, does our sense of waking vision require a necessary time of adjustment. For the waking eye always wants to render the images and words before it as individuated entities with clearly demarcated boundaries. But our method of observation here in this bedroom must be altered. If we are to read the images drifting upward from the somnolent body of Merle Haggard, then we must become acclimated to their elusive logic. They appear before us now as musical notes upon an ethereal scale. We follow their lead, remaining sensitive to the rhythm there established, the melodious patterns there wandering, and the heartstrings there shuttering in the darkness of the bedroom. Our step remains light as we take another step closer. Our gaze remains charitable, for we do not want to impose our waking language upon that mysterious language forming itself before us. We smile, remembering an old tune and the fond memories that attach themselves to it. And now, once our own breathing has been matched to his, we are ready to turn our attention to the act of decoding the dream substance of Merle Haggard.

We begin, as all interpretations should begin, with a nocturnal setting, among friendly faces and the holistic integration of a honky-tonk, a setting in which finally, after a long day of labor, a drinking man may state his problem straight and simple, without fear of scornful reprisal:

> Each night I leave the bar-room when it's over,
> not feeling any pain at closing time.
> But tonight your memory found me much too sober.
> I couldn't drink enough to keep you off my mind.

How shall we proceed? Surely we cannot consult our distant wisemen and their recondite sayings, for they have fled this land. We are alone here with the somnolent body before us. Yet sense must be made of the song. I here want to propose childhood—perhaps the quietest time of a man's life—as a possible point of entry. For childhood is a time of naming: a boy names a pet, his hunting rifle, his baseball glove, his first guitar. In the memory, however, all these names persist only as instantaneous flames flitting upward from the dreamer's head, enmeshed, attached as though at the hips with an object here in the present, and sometimes dripping with other names no longer recognized as landmarks of affection upon the strange and ever-receding horizons of memory. The central image of the song—the bottle—is one such object:

> Tonight the bottle let me down,
> and let your memory come around.
> The one true friend I thought I'd found;
> tonight the bottle let me down.

We all know how the glassy bottle feels to the fleshy lips and know the deep thirst which the bottle's contents sink down through the throat to meet, satisfy, and abide with. This liquid—whether whiskey, pilsner, juice, milk, or some combination thereof—is itself contained in the bottle and must be liberated from that glassy prison with a tip back of the head, an intrepid suck at the mouth, a satisfying swallow down the throat. And once this has been done, we lay our dollar bill upon the mahogany bar top, order another, and say to ourselves with dream-inspired confidence: the bottle, yes, this must be the bottle. Look at how it is shaped, look at how plump it is, look at how my mind and heart are satisfied when I take it into my mouth, all country-song tears wiped away, the mind cleared, the mouth busy.

It is not the bottle, of course. No, it is the maternal breast. We whisper this to ourselves—for we do not want to wake old Merle—not as a condemnation but as friends familiar with the subterranean estimation of such cravings. Then we creep a little closer to the bed. The infant's lips are at work, and we hear the next lines, hear them sweeping like a blanket over the reclining body of the venerable country singer before us:

> I've always had a bottle I could turn to,
> and lately I've been turning every day.
> But the booze don't take effect the way it used to,
> and I'm hurting in an old familiar way.

Shall we here name the partial object of desire—the breast, the booze, and the soft feather-light vowels that tie the two together in consolation? There are old familiar ways indeed. And then there is the oldest, the most familiar way, which makes use of the lexical echo in the words *familiar*, *filiation*, from the Latin *filius*, or *son*, and the mother that makes the distinction meaningful.

And what of this mother? We have her before us, too: her shirt is open, her flesh soft, while her own lips hum some soothing tune, which wraps us up like the darkness here in

Merle's bedroom. We become lightheaded, as our bellies fill, and we swish the whiskey or beer around in our mouths, thinking to ourselves that, yes, it is a painful realization that we, dear reader, have been left with no true friend and left, alas, far, far too sober.

At the riverside the next morning, I dipped my cupped hands into the water to drink. One answer to the loneliness of creation is that it always exacts from us a debt at once singular and impossible to name, and so we imagine a creator who can receive a payment that will forever elude the grip of definition. Glories entertain the illusions of the dream, but the day of reckoning comes. And there are all kinds of currencies with which to pay: song, heartbreak, liquor, dance. We send it all down the river, knowing that whatever we're sending will arrive where it is supposed to arrive, in the open mouth of whatever vague elemental ocean god or sinister snake charmer might be responsible, slipping from the mad yawning mouth of chaos, out along the sensitive forked tongue of the firmament. That is what gives the river its voice: all the sediment breaking, colliding, and chipping away at larger obstructions.

Downstream a few large boulders and deadfalls complicate its flow. Even when we pull away from the camp, to move along the highway in his Firebird, and I am sitting beside John, listening to him talk, listening also to the night and engine together collude to form a sedative of unadulterated motion, even then this complication draws me toward the river, as a question to be answered or a song to be heard, taken as blood is taken, released as an empty bottle releases all staggering humanity that needs to be eased down into that blushing substance between the ether trimming the indefinite abstraction of the horizon and the fire not yet ignited at the center of the earth, that middle and momentary ground of asphalt tempered for impact. Yet the river moves on, cradling what it can, banishing what it must. We move as it moves, down the highway, on the way to the Gas-n-Go, or to Old Man Lory's at night when the liquor has run out. And each of us is alone, confronting the thought that this valley lacks the breath of life, and that the motion of the fire is only a hollow mimicry of the consummation of blood, by blood.

Two

A BROKEN BOTTLE, AN EMPTY HEART, AND YOU'RE STILL ON MY MIND

One night after the next morning John said that he could see beneath the surface of the river. I had never seen any of the congregants ever get close to the water. Nor had I ever seen any of them walk the path that I walked each morning, just those fifty yards, down through the woods to the river's edge. Sometimes they wandered into the woods, or out onto the road, but they stayed away from the water. I think they were maybe afraid of it, and that fear surged up in their eyes the way abandon might surge up not as tears but as something close to tears the closer we approach the moment of flight.

John's claim that he could see beneath the surface of the water struck me as plainly wrong. I knew, without knowing why, the stony impossibility of the thing. If the river were translucent, then it could be felt inside as it spilled through the guts, and it would mean you could submerge your body in it the way Nathaniel did, and not withhold from its watery grip your every inner cavity, lungs, and soul. It would mean you could fill your cup and commune with the water that fills it, too.

I watched the flames of the campfire as I listened to him reason through the river, plummet its depths, disturb its surface logic. The flames flared up and descended with the strange lift and pull of his voice. I looked around; the congregants, too, were staring into the fire. They maybe even thought it was now the fire that was addressing them.

John raised himself up off the faded quilt we were sitting on and asked out loud, to no one in particular, how long we thought it would take the fire to eat through the thin flesh of a can of beer. Then he turned to one of his congregants, more audience than spectator at this time of night, and asked him to fetch him a drink.

The kid returned with an armful of cans and emptied them all out on a blanket, tossing one over to John. John caught it in midair, and exhibited it to us. He turned to the fire and threw the unopened can of beer into the embers. There was a moment of silence as the flames licked their way around this new provision. Then there was more talk about a glimmer evidencing an invisible captive beneath the surface of the Hiwassee water—it was thought, he announced, pure thought—that had been lodged there in the sluice that flowed past us night after night, or the same night, and always the next morning, but his talk was subdued by the creeping flames into which his hearers stared.

I tried to locate the can among the glowing sticks and the coals that pulsated with the bright orange waves of heat, but I could not. John was still staring down into the fire, crouching there, his hands on his knees, upturned as though to find there a silence more decisive than the heartbreaking silence of the starry night itself.

Then just like that, he bent down and reached his hand into the flames. It was a slow unwavering motion in, and a slow unwavering motion out. He popped open the can of beer, tipped his head back and drained it in a single draught. He held the empty can up to the flame, to me, to everyone else, and he said the flame cannot eat the body. It eats the spirit, the translucent fluid that animates the body, but never the body itself. What does it care about the flesh, the aluminum, the asphalt, the vessel, the chrome, the brake, the chassis? Then he dropped the can to the ground and said that it was the same for the river over there. Seeing through it does not make it any easier to touch.

There is nothing other than thirst to make us look downstream, where the river narrows, the current becomes swifter, and the sediment takes on more force. But upstream, the water is tranquil.

The next morning I woke and walked away from them all still sleeping there and went down to the river to wash my mouth out. I saw him there, Nathaniel, on the other side. He stripped off his shirt and pants and waded into the water, leaving his clothes in a small heap beside a tree. His head bobbed in the current. Then he dipped under the surface, and a deer from the shadows crept along the bank on the far side. The cautious creature looked up from the brambles and weeds before taking another step. It paused then darted off.

John always says that drunks not only dream about water but some of them can also breathe it the way they sometimes breathe liquor, the evidence of which comes from the well-known fact that they don't need to take in any air when they are pulling up or tipping back a long one. Such are the analytic powers of the mind, he would say, and point to his mouth. The thinking mouth.

The image is not impossible. And there is Nathaniel at the bottom of the river, maybe whistling a tune. He belches underwater and pockets of air ascend. They have messages contained in them. Like hellfire a moment too soon or the graven dust of heaven an hour too late, John sometimes says when we're driving down the highway in his Firebird. Maybe his thoughts could have been counted instead of the seconds. There he is, in his own element, slowed current, catfish watching with their greased smiles. The weeds move underwater like the tentacles of something alive, but bearing no name. He breathes in, then out, and the water's color changes.

The mind a mouth of its own. For John, though, it's the other way around: the mouth a mind of its own.

There is not a single step taken forward, Evenene, padded feet against the padded forest floor, nor a single strike of the steel of the imagination against the blunt and leaden edge of the woods.

There is nothing that can root out the finessed attunements of the singing swallow, the chirping robin, or the calling jay. For the imagination sharpens itself against names only, and the names that have swayed the bird to the cusp of his song have their jagged origin in some broken bottle not one of us has yet to drink from. Sure there are traces of feathers, prints in the mud, the remains of ancient crushed shells—but it's the names that stick, clinging as they do to the thin air or as cloud mounts upon cloud and mile upon hour.

I have sat for hours after waking the next morning and watched him sleep it off, the woods behind him, surrounding our camp, collecting itself into a single entity and standing against him, spiteful of our movements here where nothing else moves except the river and occasionally the heavy summer boughs in the breeze. The woods are a barrier that silence cannot break, but two silences cannot remain so close, either. The woods can eat but cannot thrive off of mere sparks, cannot remain satisfied with those immolated specks of itself, settling to the ground, for ash is already a consumed thing. The sylvan forces see in ash an image of their own starved double. But the woods also eat the crushed aluminum and glass bottles we hurl into the shadows at night, in the morning, in the afternoon out the car window when we're driving from nowhere to nowhere in the Firebird.

When John sleeps he is not a thinking thing. Or if he is, so is the mountain to the east of us. I had heard somewhere that Old Man Lory used to go up that very same mountain. At night, when we sit drinking in his garage among the carcasses of the car exposed beneath the open hood and raised up on cinder blocks, I try to decode his talk about his communion with the mountain. I imagine him saying that the mountain told him he was no longer welcome. The mountain is a thinking thing, the clouds its thoughts, and I could picture the old man making it up halfway one morning, taking a deep breath, pausing at a crest, gazing up out of some glade, and reading the message clearly, without protesting the hard injustice of it, aware of the fact that his body had finished with the mountain, too, and that probably a few hunting seasons ago. The two could part with no hard feelings. It does no good to curse the mountain for its incline, but its words, high above, are its own. And they are law.

We were on the road again. Trailing behind us were the other cars and pickups. The Gas-n-Go was our destination, where Reggie would fill us all up, the cars with gasoline, the backseats and trunks and truck beds with cold beer, cigarettes, chew, flowers, coffee, coolant, radiator fluid, candy, and gum for those who still had the taste for it—anything any of them wanted—it was all for our taking.

Beside us was the river. John thinks the river is a sneering lie. It cuts through the landscape so far back that no one can protest it any longer and takes with its current all the filth that had escaped the grip of the mountain. It reflects the sky but lacks the guts to swallow it. I believe John loves that river because he considers it a curse perfected long ago, never having wavered from its course, its path being established and never questioned ever since the first drop of water tumbled down the mountain, into the valley here, taking the path of least resistance, down, down, through the lush and varied landscape, before the eyes of all the animals who could not catch it with their tongues.

We drove on, enveloped in the sound of the engine. The paved ground beneath us seemed to draw everything to it. There is no escape from the absolute statement the road makes with its agitated, horizontal body.

It does not contend, John said as the Firebird picked up speed, does not compete with the precision of the pistons, with their mechanical commitment to each end of the shaft, nor with any of the engined ideas residing deep within the guts of the polished, greased, half-drunk body pumping out friendship into one another by night, Evenene, and piercing the humid totality by day, with this forward assertion of mine, and with the beautiful hammer-hard looks you give this world, Jenny, in the pursuit of what can only be won with speed and drink, what can only be gained for one day alone before retreating into the recesses of sleep, with its monotone facade, its misty unconscious play, nothing momentous about a dream, nothing certain except the images that linger and sometimes cast strange shadows onto the world after waking, after saying once and for all and adding nothing more than the enduring observation that drunks dream of water. It can be no other way. Grant that and the river can't touch you, Evenene, grant that drunks dream of water and you'll quit looking for life in the trees or nourishment in the ground, or in the depths of the fire, or in the late-summer scent of rot and mulch that clings to us all.

The next morning we were on the road again, sitting in the Firebird, the noise of its engine rushing over me, as water might rush over those who have drank their fill and found sleep among the wild grass of a roadside ditch.

I have heard stories that spoke of the surface of the earth as a great, magnificent, and varied face, whose expressions change in a series of slow, gradual shifts completed over millennia, and whose lineaments are the work of geologic forces never at rest.

The valley here is defined to the east by the mountain. It towers over us, not as a feature of the landscape but as a singularity, an entity, some living substance that had risen up in defiance of whatever subterranean moods had given form and expression to the surface. Seen at this hour in mid-morning, the mountain blends in with the sky, but the vagueness of its outline only furthers the clarity of its single thought.

And what is that single thought? I do not yet know, but I know that it has been preparing its pronouncement for a long time, maybe for all time. Every trembling geologic murmur, every footstep of every creature that has crept upon it, every collision of lightning and thunder, and the whole chorus of raindrops pounding into its mud—all of this it will gather up and fashion into a single voice when the hour ripens and it comes time to deliver its judgment.

John once told me that the peak of the mountain emerged long ago as a ghastly eye on the landscape, when it was driven by pride to stare directly into the noontime sun. This ancient and elemental longing of the earth caused it to quake in its depths and rise up. But when it looked directly into the sun, it was blinded, and the mountain cried out for relief. The earth heard the cry of this fugitive and arrogant mountain and sent the west wind to dry out the fluids of its eye, but the eye was protected by a series of great cathedral-like rock formations, against which the west wind vainly pounded for thirty days and thirty nights before finally abandoning the task.

Then all the animals heard the cry of the mountain, but only a few could muster the courage to scale its heights—the mountain lion, big horn sheep, and some others—but none of those had an ear for the distress of stone, and each went his separate way.

It was at this time that the rarest of all the animals, the phoenix, happened to be passing by. He heard the lament of the blind mountain and, swooping down through the rocks that circumscribed it, went to investigate. His fiery wing brushed the surface of the strange substance that had formed over the eye, and, flammable, it immediately caught fire, and continued to burn for ages after.

But to behold a small fire close up is the same as beholding the great fire of the sun from a great distance, and the mountain no longer had to look away. The gelatinous machinery of its geologic vision—the great rods and cones and prisms—melted into a liquid substance, what we would now call gasoline—and that great lake of fire continued to burn. They say that it can still be seen on moonless nights flickering between the jagged stones that surround it.

Other versions of the story claim that it wasn't that the mountain rose in defiance of the earth for a glimpse of the sun. It's that the sun fell in love with the earth once and wanted to possess it. But the earth in her telluric wisdom knew that if any communion between her body and the body of the sun occurred, she would be swallowed up and immolated along with all the life that had sprung from her soil. So she called to herself the four winds, north, east, west, and south, whose wisdom exceeded everything else by virtue of their having travelled the whole wide world. She explained her problem and sought their counsel.

After some deliberation, it was decided that a gift would be given to appease the lust of the sun and thereby escape the inevitable annihilation that would otherwise occur if that lust were to be realized upon her body. And so the four winds were sent away to gather up the most precious gifts they could find. They returned sometime later and gathered in an open field in order to present to the sun what they had found. The north was the first. He offered rich red wine, and when the sun accepted it, he became drunk and this only further inflamed his desire, and so out of either elation or spite, he permitted the only animal who had ever looked up at him—the human animal—the sole proprietorship of this substance by virtue of excluding all the other animals from feeling both its delights and sorrows.

The next gift, from the west, was blood. But as the chalice that contained the gift was being handed over, the sun fumbled the exchange and the blood spilled over the rocks and stones.

Seeing it flow, the sun became fascinated with its appearance there and created ritual sacrifice, bitter wars, car wrecks, and virginity.

The next was the east, and he offered the sun thick, white, creamy milk. But the milk warmed when the sun accepted it and, after he had swallowed it down, he became sleepy and dreamed of the great, soft bosom of the earth. When he woke, he placed it in the breast of womankind so that she could nourish her young with similar dreams of solace.

Finally, the west wind, the subtlest and most taciturn of the four winds, stepped forward with his gift. He presented the oil of a rock, known as petroleum. It was viscous and black, and the sun, upon receiving the gift, recognized in this color the image of the night, which, true, he had never before seen with his own eyes, but who, he knew, was the only other cosmic force as powerful as he was. He seized the vessel of petroleum to cast it off to the side, but when he came into contact with it, the substance blazed up and his image was doubled there before him. He became consumed by this image of himself and stared silently into the flames that arose from the burning crude oil.

When the flame went out, he demanded more, and more was brought, and when that had burned, he demanded yet more and still more was delivered. The sun remained fixed in place, contemplating the image of himself there, forgetting his lust for the earth, but also forgetting his duty to journey from horizon to horizon. Time stopped, as a result, and with it the various cyclical processes that maintained order upon the earth. Perhaps the most disturbing effect of this suspension of time was the cessation of the decompositional process: without any progression of time, the corpses of the many animals and plants that relied upon its hand to reintegrate and transform into new material configurations remained littered upon the land, leading their poisons down into its once fertile ground, and choked up the channels of the great rivers that fed the sea.

Surveying her body thus defiled, she buried the black crude oil deep within her, piled mountain and sea upon it. At the same time, she instructed men about how to retrieve it from her depths and, to elude the appetite of the sun, taught them a trick to refine it into a transparent liquid called gasoline. She told the sun to return the next day and there would be more, and each day the sun passes in hopes of getting a glimpse of that crude oil atop the mountain.

I leaned back in the passenger seat and watched the sun sign itself with the shadows of the leafy boughs onto the windshield. I felt the terrible engine idling beneath me. The cars of the congregants were also idling in the camp, and a great roar ascended up from there.

John shoved it into first, and the car lurched forward over the small dirt mound that separated the grassy section on which we parked from the highway. We were on the road then, heading for the Gas-n-Go. The congregation sped up and paralleled us. One who was riding in the bed of a pickup threw an empty beer bottle against the road sign that flashed by. From the truck they hollered and gestured with their hands, accelerating and decelerating wildly as we all caravanned down the road. One of the faster cars among them—a Nova—sped past us. I caught a glimpse of the two kids in the back seat, each staring out the window, as I was staring out mine.

The one nearest to me was smoking a cigarette, and I could see the thin trail of smoke rushing out of the open window, then vanish the moment it hit the force of the open road, as all things vanish there. I thought of that smoke, dissipating in the air over the paved highway for a moment, as it separated, the deceitful symmetry of the invisible warmth of the sun doing its work to drive wedges between even the most ethereal of bodies, and knew then why the work of the engine had to be covered by the hood, hidden from the ridicule and disintegrating powers of the daylight, and I thought about the nebulous flesh that separates thought from its material conditions—the epidermal insult to all that feels itself compelled to fly upward and re-congregate in the air, as dust, sheer abstracted speed, as fiery bird, as piston steam.

Dust, they say, is slow, and I have heard of great silences, of geologic calms, mythopoetic hushes, rapturous voids and theologic tranquilities, all broken open in a single collision of thought and deed. I have heard stories that explained the meaning of the bright spot between the eyes, which some call consciousness and others call awareness and which yet others call miles per hour, rotations per second, or pounds per inch, or a whole host of other names that hang suspended in the air of our country tunes, and despite these thousand names spilling into the night above the highway, everyone beholds in those names the key to such mysteries as cause and effect, formal identity, action and reaction, faith and doubt, truth and falsehood. That bright spot between the eyes is hooded by the work of dreams, dreams of water for the drunkard, dreams of riches for the poor, dreams of flight for the animals.

And what do the animals know? I once heard that the bright spot between the eyes is for the animals a brightness suffused over their entire body, near the tongue when the doe licks the placenta off its newborn, around the tongue when the old wolf licks the blade of the knife stuck in the snow, licks his own blood, which inflames a hunger that is co-extensive with the brightness that covers his whole panting howling body, and that teaches the creature how to die, glutted on his own blood from the upright blade, without the panic or the corporeal squalor that characterizes the human being's final break with sight, sound, smell, touch, and taste. The animals do not need to keep that brightness behind their eyes because their eyes have never needed to know where the moonlight was coming from, their mouths and ears never touched words but let them pass by on the breeze or on the surface of the water, their tongues as indifferent to steel as to ice as to blood as to the drip between legs and the rot far beneath the layer of dead leaves on the forest floor, down in the woods' loam, the finery of its seasonal layers an inadequate mask for the trace of the great obscene human heart that sits mawkish and sweating fireballs at the center of the earth, where it believes itself to have found its own hiding place from the eyes of the buzzards who fly above it all.

Reginald Hawkins Braddard,
Gasoline Station Attendant, Is Dead at 59

Reginald Hawkins Braddard, an attendant at Victor's Gas-n-Go off Highway 27 for thirty-seven years, died early Monday morning just north of Graysville.

The cause of death was cerebral hemorrhage, said the examiner at Rhea County Hospital in Dayton. After finishing his lunch, Mr. Braddard lit a cigarette, opened a can of RC Cola, and collapsed from the wooden stool on which he most often sat. The proprietor of the Gas-n-Go, Martin Victor, was alarmed by the sound of the crash and rushed outside to find his employee "crawling toward the pumps," with one hand against the back of his head. When the paramedics appeared twenty minutes later, Mr. Braddard was pronounced dead upon arrival.

The Gas-n-Go boasted of being the only service station between Dayton and Chattanooga open twenty-four hours a day. Braddard could often be found in the early morning hours into the late hours of the night sitting outside on his stool when weather permitted and in inclement weather sitting inside gazing out the window for approaching customers. His expertise in handling the pumps and his extensive knowledge of the crucial differences between unleaded gas, premium unleaded gas, regular, and diesel fuel made him indispensable, said Victor.

Capable conversation skills allowed Mr. Braddard to entertain and inform a wide array of customers. His advice in mechanics often fell upon the sympathetic ears of truckers moving shipments along Highway 27, as did his insights into schedule and location of the speed traps set up by the state patrol. Having grown up in the area, Mr. Braddard earned a reputation as a reliable source for directions to out-of-town vacationers and local travelers alike.

"His general know-how when it came to where you're at will certainly be missed," said one frequenter of Victor's Gas-n-Go.

Mr. Braddard was respected for his often insightful commentary on such well-known television shows as *Combat!* and *I Love Lucy*. "He was sharp," said another customer who knew Braddard, "No doubt about it. Didn't say much though. But you always knew he was thinking."

Reginald Hawkins Braddard was born on March 10, 1918, in Riceville, Tennessee and moved to Graysville when still a teenager. He spent two years in Graysville Elementary and at the age of fifteen signed on with the Searlen Katz Coal Co. where he worked six days a week throughout the 1930s. In 1942 he suffered an injury to the left hand that rendered him unemployable in the mines and disallowed him from joining the military, as many of his former co-workers had done in subsequent years.

Later that year, Victor employed Mr. Braddard for a small salary and provided housing for his single employee. "It was the provision of accommodations," remembers one regular customer who knew Braddard well. "That was what appealed to him most."

The contents of the small, single-bedroom house located in the back lot behind the station will go up for sale next month. A public auction will be held for Mr. Braddard's belongings, which include a fifteen-inch color television, an antique coin collection and a Ford Mustang frame with a 312 CID Ford V6 engine, and a new transmission.

"He always talked about getting her fixed up," said Victor.

Mr. Braddard is survived by an aunt in Rutherford County, Emma Vera, and a second cousin in Nashville, Lloyd Turner.

Victor said Reginald was fond of talking about his family in the big city. "When folks from Nashville would pass through and stopped for gas, Reggie would always ask them if they knew a Mr. Lloyd Turner, that smile of his broadening into a shy grin as he said the name."

You see we are all a subterranean force, he was saying, morningside, riverside, fireside, driverside, all things to all these beautiful people, slamming their goddamn brains against the vanities of automotive life, against a meager paycheck, a lovesick song, tumbling from that engine with the brow-beating promise of a thousand crows, having never bathed except in blood. John was fully drunk now, taking the curves fast, developing his cheap and easy curse into something luxurious, inquiring with a threatening look whether or not those figurative crows he had just conjured out of his enthusiastic spite of the daylight had in fact ever known woman as anything but a slick and leaky open corpse two three four days ripe, if they had ever known cities as anything other than eternally burning and absolutely random arrangements of shipyards, battlefields, prison yards, cornfields, front yards, back yards, steel mills, paper mills, saw mills, brick, tar, and gravel, and if the crushed people there could be ground down to a finer dust that the crows might use to blacken the brow above the midnight black centers of their eyes.

The next morning after I'd woke up before them all, we went for a ride for food and drink to the Gas-n-Go. Thirst is not to be doubted, John was saying as he pulled into Vic's. It is a claw that holds you in its sharp and deadly sway. Thirst sometimes is the only way our body speaks for itself, when it is not in the favor of words, when the two are opposed to one another as the body—chassis and panels—of the car is opposed to its engine.

Reggie set down his RC and came over to the car. He yanked the pump off the hook and weighed it for a moment in his good hand. The long nozzle looked like the beak of some bird. With his elbow he hit the switch, and there was that hollow gurgle of the gas going in. Beyond the gas station there was a field, and beyond that trees. Somewhere the eye could not go, too, was the river, and I thought of the claim it had made on us, merely by having one day long ago lain its long sleek body down in this valley.

Then I saw Nathaniel. He was standing near the entrance of the gas station, leaning against the wall. No one else among us seemed to see him. The other kids passed by directly in front of him without taking notice of his presence. Some of the others were already inside, standing at the counter, wandering around the isles, talking, gesturing to one another toward their purchases. But Nathaniel was not watching them either. His gaze was fixed in my direction, and when Reggie stood up from his wooden stool to fetch another cola, I realized that it was he whom Nathaniel had been watching.

He would not even know about the pet canary that flew freely through the small interior of the Gas-n-Go and sometimes perched itself on the cash register or hopped along the bottom of the window sill. I once saw that bird eat from Reggie's good hand. It had been raining outside, and John and I had gone inside to pay Vic. Reggie followed us and shook himself of the rain, stomped the mat that lay at the threshold. He whistled, maybe at the storm outside, or at the wet linoleum inside. The canary was flying around in a panic, from one shelf to another. Then it flew over to Reggie, alighting on his mangled hand. Reggie, with his good hand, yanked the cigarette out of his mouth, turned it in his fingers and carefully ashed in his palm. The canary leapt there and pecked at the ash until it crumbled. He likes doing that, Reggie said to us. I was wondering if the bird had swallowed any of it.

Reginald Hawkins Braddard, Gasoline Station Attendant, Is Dead at 59

Reginald Hawkins Braddard, an attendant at Victor's Gas-n-Go off Highway 27 for thirty-seven years, died early Monday morning just north of Graysville.

The cause of death was cerebral hemorrhage, said the examiner at Rhea County Hospital in Dayton. After finishing his lunch, Mr. Braddard lit a cigarette, opened a can of RC Cola, and collapsed from the wooden stool on which he most often sat. The proprietor of the Gas-n-Go, Martin Victor, was alarmed by the sound of the crash and rushed outside to find his employee "crawling toward the pumps," with one hand in the air clutching a small yellow canary thought to be Mr. Braddard's pet. According to Victor, the canary did not fly from the man's grip even after he had lost consciousness. "It was waiting for him to wake," said Victor. When the paramedics arrived twenty minutes later, Mr. Braddard was pronounced dead.

While the origin of the canary was unknown, it had enjoyed a certain acclaim in the minds of many of the frequenters of the Gas-n-Go. Mr. Braddard had trained it to perform various tricks, including one in which the canary would fetch a piece of peppermint candy, carry it back to Mr. Braddard in its beak and deposit it in his open hand. The trick was a favorite among children.

Mr. Braddard was known for his ability to whistle. While at the pumps, he often instructed children how to purse the lips, blow air, the precise arrangement of the fingers in the mouth. "Any tune you could name," said one customer of the station, "and he could whistle it. Just like that."

His repertoire for whistling increased significantly when the station purchased its first television set, Victor remembers. Mr. Braddard's knowledge of television show tunes was often put to the test by his customers. Challenges would often come from all ages, and all were invariably impressed by Braddard's talents.

Reginald Hawkins Braddard was born on March 10, 1918, in Riceville, Tennessee and moved to Graysville when still a teenager. He spent two years in Graysville Elementary and at the age of fifteen signed on with the Searlen Katz Coal Co. where he worked six days a week throughout the 1930s. In 1942 he suffered an injury to the left hand that rendered him unemployable in the mines. The coal company kept him on the payroll, however, and put him to work caring for the brood of canaries kept by the miners for the detection of methane and carbon monoxide.

An incident ensued between Mr. Braddard and management, apparently involving the canaries and the former's refusal to send them into a new seam. After one such altercation, Mr. Braddard was promptly released.

Later that year, Victor employed Mr. Braddard for a small salary and provided housing for his single employee. "It was the provision of accommodations," remembers one regular customer who knew Braddard well. "That was what appealed to him most."

The contents of the small, single-bedroom house located out in the back lot behind the station will go up for sale next month. A public auction will be held for Mr. Braddard's belongings, which include a fifteen-inch color television, and a Ford Mustang frame with a 312 CID Ford V6, a new transmission, and a large ornate bird cage appraised at a considerable value.

"I'd never known him to keep anything but old newspapers in it," said Victor.

Mr. Braddard is survived by an aunt in Rutherford County, Emma Vera, and a second cousin in Nashville, Lloyd Turner.

Victor said Reginald was fond of talking about his family in the big city. When folks from Nashville passed through and stop for gas, Reggie would whistle in amazement and remark on the great distance they must have traveled.

The next morning on the bank of the river I felt the cold slide up under my thin nightgown and woke before the rest of them. I took a blanket up off the ground and wrapped it around my shoulders. I stepped down the path to the edge of the river and kneeled. I cupped my hands and dipped them down into the cold water then splashed it on my face. It was still early.

A thin layer of mist hung above the water. Neither the mist nor the water moved. But it must move. The water moves down from the mountain to wash us out, even at an hour this early, glides over the bodies of the fish, among the stalks of the cattail and riverweed, over stones and through the valley, too fast to be captured by the drowsy mind of Nathaniel, and so he just lay there on the ground. The water smoothes the stones at the bottom of the river, sculpts the muddy banks, weighs the deadfalls with a new density that they had not possessed in their long-lost days of uprightness.

We look east and think about where the water has come from. We look west and think about where the water is going. From the head of the sleeper flow palpitant images of water. It rains, and the river grows. It does not rain and the river recedes. But the river did not begin with rain. Water from a mountain spring begins deep within the earth. The water accumulates and ascends up through the limestone, granite, soft black soil, up through the annual padding of dead leaves. Once the water has found the surface, it issues down the mountain, creeping along at the lowest point. It collects in the small palm of a brittle leaf until it spills over the edge and finds a larger leaf to fill. It then pools over the edge and finds a bed of stone, where it waits to gather more of its disparate body together, before falling over the cusp of whatever contains it and sliding further down the mountain.

It was not a difficult process to describe but, like so much else in this place, I could not easily account for my knowing it. What is it sleep does if not cover the body each night, and how can something as diaphanous as the memory stand in for something as heavy and solid and enveloping as sleep?

The highway at night does not vanish, nor do we. There is no flash, no sudden commerce between the body of the car and the road, between the speed, fuel, and music streaming from the car speakers. When the eyes open onto the world, the world is there to greet them. Has it been waiting, somewhere in the tricky substance of the next morning?

John says that all the birds are asleep, underneath the hood of his Trans Am, that they have given up their feathery bodies and assumed a more meaningful kind of flight, having merged into a single force now to break open the melodies and harmonies of the country tunes surging from the stereo speakers there, or the parts under the hood of the Trans Am, united into a totality that cannot be divided without being broken.

It is the possibility of never having to touch the ground that makes the figure of the bird so appealing to John. But it must be conceived as a living thing because, alive, it is able to eat away at the grandiose image that it makes upon that hood and in John's twilighting imagination. For the birds are conversant with elevations that free them from having to breathe the same air as those inferior land-dwelling creatures.

A curse must be dressed up as something beautiful if it is not to fall on deaf ears, and the image of the bird embodies this kind of curse. The bird does all that a curse should be able to do: encase itself in a body that can elude the eye, shatter the glass of the windshield, eat from the hand. That it might fly away and never return only enriches its allure.

To never step on the same bit of earth twice, he once said, is a bullshit lie if the earth you've got beneath your feet has been spilled from your own guts or been flattened by asphalt. For the first time ever since the world first skidded onto the open road, there have so far been none to walk it, until now. This patch of ground, whether coughed up in an act of compassion or cruelty, might not have the expansiveness of the deer's eye, or of the buzzard's gut, but there is great generosity in its refusal to give us peace.

From the plush green grass at the bank of the river I watched Nathaniel. He lay motionless on his back. The tall grass concealed much of his body. There was an opening in the trees above him. The sun was coming up but had not yet reached the horizon. The mountain to the east of here cast its long shadow over our valley.

When daylight finally came, it arrived shrill and sudden. At the edge of my field of vision, far above the tops of the trees that formed the opening above the man reclining on the far side of the river, I saw something move. It was a buzzard. It wheeled around, slowly on its shaky axis, wings spread, tilting on the currents of air.

I had nothing to gain by thinking of birds as material expressions of John's thoughts. He had claimed to see them, claimed even to have hitched a ride on one up to the top of the mountain one night after the rest of us had passed out, the fire had died down, and he sat finishing his drink alone.

He told me that an enormous buzzard had appeared the very moment he drained the last drop of the last beer in camp. The buzzard landed fifty yards off or so and waited in the darkness. After John had rummaged through blankets, coolers, and weeds, searching for booze by firelight, the buzzard stepped forward and surveyed the camp. He asked what was the matter. John told him he was thirsty. The buzzard said he knew of a place up at the top of the mountain that held all kinds of liquor, beer, you name it.

John hates the mountain and he told the buzzard this, adding that he was not in the mood for a walk through the woods in the middle of the night, especially not without the necessary assuaging libations. The buzzard laughed and spread his enormous wings, emphasizing his great size, then hobbled awkwardly the way buzzards will, coming closer to the fire, and offered to escort him to the top. But John doubted the stamina of the bird. In fact, John later told me, the intentions of that vile beast were suspect from the start. Yet the prospect of more booze demanded at least some consideration.

Thinking of the long night of solitude and the merciless, creeping sobriety ahead of him, he eventually agreed to the buzzard's offer. His suspicion remained, and so he devised a plan that he thought would ensure his safety. He asked the bird for a moment to prepare himself for the journey and, when the bird complied, John snuck off into the shadows of the woods beyond the firelight. In the dark, he felt on the ground for the largest stones he could find and filled a sack with them. Once it was full, he returned to the camp and jumped onto the back of the buzzard. The great beast turned to him and said that he seemed heavier than he appeared. John answered that it was often that way with the human body—such a frail thing, a joke really, until you have to carry one around with you. Nevertheless, the stately and grotesque bird said, it is a manageable burden.

Now it is not an easy thing for a turkey vulture to initiate flight. His large wings, weak legs, and general awkwardness on the ground make leaving the surface of the earth rather difficult. The bird hops forward to gain momentum, pushing off the ground with his feet, all the while flapping his wings laboriously, huffing, puffing, hissing, grunting. And so it was with this great buzzard, only the effort was now intensified by the human body he carried on his back.

After a rough start, the bird caught the air beneath his wings and ascended into the night, leaving the camp, the silent parked cars, the aggravated firelight. John clung to the bird's feathers and stole a look around. He could see the tavern, he said, which was empty now, the last few patrons of the bar having stumbled out many hours ago. He could see the Gas-n-Go, with its neon sign illuminating the small stretch of highway before it. He even ventured a look back toward the river, a faint snaking figure whose beginning and end lay beyond the reach of this lofty perspective. He could see the road, too, which paralleled the river, but circled back in on itself, and in the center of its coils was the campsite, its firelight a small spark in the vast night. They flew on, and John took all of this in.

As they climbed, so, too, did the mountain climb in the east, enormous, growing larger as the great buzzard approached it. Everything was deathly silent, of course. The buzzard soared on the thermals rising up from the earth. Occasionally the meditative swoosh of the wings broke the lofty hush that surrounded them in flight. The only other sound was the low wheeze of the bird's giant lungs as they took in the air, laying down a solid and meditative rhythm which John could feel alter the shape of the buzzard's body.

At one point in their gradual ascent, John reached into his bag, pulled out a stone and dropped it into the void below him. As they drew closer to the mountain, climbing higher and higher, John dropped another stone, then another, off the side of the strange living vehicle he clung to, and the moment he released them with his hand was the last moment of contact—for he could neither see nor hear them once they had left his grip. And thus the buzzard was unburdened from the weight of the load, and was able to press on without feeling his powers diminish.

Finally, the mountain surrounded the entire field of vision, and the bird began his descent. It was a dramatic shift, one John felt in his body, and he instinctively gripped the bird's feathers more tightly. Just before cresting the pinnacle of the mountain, the buzzard dove, stiffened his neck and jerked his body downward, in rapid descent through the tops of the trees. The great creature then spread his wings to catch the air and slowed his momentum, touching finally the ground, catching it under his feet with a rough, blundering series of steps forward and a great flapping of his wings.

John, by his own account, had sobered up considerably by now, and he wanted to savor more deeply the thrilling experience he had just had on the back of the bird with something to drink, a cold beer maybe or a pull of whiskey. He surveyed the area in the faint gray light of the pre-dawn hours. The top of the mountain was just slightly less dramatic than the journey there. He could see far beyond the river, to the west into the valley where lights of cities with no destination glimmer faintly.

He told me he saw nothing but woods and open road, that there was nothing on that other side we don't have here, Jenny. From the top of the mountain he could see our highway, too, winding alongside the river at some places, breaking off into open expanses at others, then dense roadside forest, paralleling narrow hedgerow, could see the road assert its endlessness against the frailty of the human eye, and against the stupor of those who might have the folly and gutlessness of wanting a destination to put an end to the pavement. In both directions, John said, the road outran the ability of the eye to capture it.

He turned away from the beautiful sight there at the lofty heights of the mountain and looked at the buzzard, perched on a nearby boulder. John approached him and smiled. It is lovely up here, he said, in fact, so lovely that the only way to improve the high, rarified beauty of this place would be to enjoy it with one of those drinks you promised me. The buzzard stared at the man before him, emitted a great sigh of despair. Then, shaking his head, he said that if you need some kind of further intoxication than the intoxicating heights to which I have just introduced your frail human lungs, those majestic sights that my hard work and generosity have afforded you, if human thirst cannot be satisfied with such rarified beauty, and if the human body desires poison after such pure air, then that body is destined to putrefy alone in the field, sufficiently cursed to keep even me away.

Nathaniel still had not moved. From my side of the river I could see the suggestion of a few more buzzards above, holding a scattered yet coherent pattern in the sky with patience and the subtlety fit for the creature who eats away the refuse, eats death itself. They were still a considerable distance away, but they were moving in.

The problem with John's story about going to the top of the mountain on a giant buzzard's back did not lie in the fantastic size of the animal or the impossibility of the confrontation between the bird and the man once the man had found out there was no liquor—a confrontation which John had said ended with his killing the beast and drinking the blood, since, Jenny, buzzards are the thoughts of the drunk man just before sleep takes over, and if you can't get drunk off what you yourself have dreamed up, then you deserve the slow crush of the duration, tossed maybe into the grass, kept face down and left for dead. No—the problem with it all had nothing to do with this. It had to do with the impossibility of John's ever going up to the top of the mountain. He would simply never do it.

The top of the mountain, and what must lie beyond it, terrifies him, because it symbolizes some kind of boundary, because he loves the void that lies at the center of this valley, and that to go over the mountain is to find an end to whatever pattern we have been holding here, each next morning when I wake, then the drive to the Gas-n-Go, the Matinee, the hill, then Old Man Lory's garage, and the descent of the night, how it comes without justification, neither suddenly nor gradually, but comes the way drunkenness sometimes comes, all at once though it's been there for a long time, back before those crisp openings of the memory have awakened in the mind the memory of light.

John hates the mountain because he knows that the mountain is the only thing that can move here. His talk is itself a feeble river because it pretends to the heights and lethargy of the mountain. If it can move, then it can close in on us, while we're driving down the highway at night maybe, or when we're sleeping in each other's arms. Maybe he senses the mountain has a pulse. Maybe it has some luminescence at its center and can take away whatever the shadows beyond the camp are hiding or whatever the inchoate flux that flies past the Firebird on the side of the highway is saying.

For I have perceived that this place speaks. But its language is not the same as that which spills from the eyes, or gets garbled in the mouths of those other kids here. Nor is it the same language of Old Man Lory and the other old men who grunt and curse from behind their cans of beer or their coffee cups full of whiskey when we sit in the garage each night near the corpse of a car propped up on cinder blocks, nor of Reggie and his mangled hand as he holds the gas pump to the car. The river and the engine of John's Trans Am—these resemble the language of waking up the next morning, and the language of the flat incoherent manifold walled up on either side of the highway at night.

And that morning when I was watching the buzzards hovering above Nathaniel as he slept, I realized, too, that it was the same broken tones of an accursed flesh, apportioned according to the sneers of the feathered living creatures above, great alar purifiers of the land, closing in now on him as they were, tilting more dramatically against the blunt azure expanse of the sky. The meaning of their advance was that things cannot remain as they are. That hovering creaturely presence is one that cannot be declaimed—nor can it be refuted. It can be watched, and that is all.

Even if the tires of the car find the confused skull of the quivering animal on the highway, it will only ever add up to a few last gasps on the part of the victim, a few whimpers in the night, muscles flinching, claws digging into the pavement for traction. It will all be met with an incomprehensibility that the body works no longer, that the machine is broken, and that the will can do nothing to repair it, and as the car speeds on, and darkness replaces the headlights' halogen glow, the lungs, the heart, the joints, the fur, the teeth of the doomed roadside kill—they will pronounce that things cannot really remain as they are.

Now the buzzard feeds off of carrion and detects the fumes emanating from a dead body in the initial stages of decay. The buzzard wants the flesh when it is whispering, not when it is crying out. And the drunk, of course, dreams of water—but water has its own role to play in the meticulous processes of decomposition. Or does it sit and ferment in the same place, exposed to the sun, to the birds in the air, so that it becomes undrinkable?

The grass Nathaniel lay on covered some of his large body, but his head was in plain sight. His mouth was open, and something wet gleamed on his upper lip. I counted five buzzards there, stationary now, wings propped open like car doors, staring at the man lying in the grass, dreaming of the river, its destination, its incessant coursing through this single vein of the earth's body.

No, it is not rain that the river first begins as. Long ago, the mountain to the east of us lifted itself up one morning after a long sleep and caused a great rush of water, of leaves, of deadwood, and dandelions, tufts of fur, lost feathers, all to tumble, then float, then cascade down the incline created by the mountain's new posture. And the water still follows this first path down, a path of least resistance, rivuleting, ricocheting, snaking through and over all that composes the mountainside. The water even bides its time and sinks deep into the ground, through the soil, to the bedrock where it accumulates and ascends up through the flakes of limestone, the granite, the decayed leaves and wood and carcass that goes into layering the forest floor, up through the earlier layers which have had the time to become more uniform, to the newer layers which might still bear the resemblance of what they were in past lives—a hint of the brittle sharp angle of a maple leaf, the exquisitely checkered cap of an acorn, a chunk of bark inscribed by the striations of lichen, all long ago fallen, getting each moment closer to the ground before joining it and becoming a part of the diminuendo chords of its affirmation.

The buzzards were as motionless as Nathaniel was. But their eyes were alert. From their beaks they emitted a low occasional grunt. Not even the birds should get too attached to the air, John says, because one day the ground will rise up to meet and swallow them. Nathaniel had still not moved, and the buzzards hopped closer. It had been a long night of drinking.

The mountains are thinking beings, the clouds their thoughts. The chicken hawk gives us a good picture of flight. But he is the only one who sees. The voice of the river does not speak with its bedrock, but with the mists that ascend up from it, invisible to all but the most careful observers. In the same way, there are beams of light that shoot from the head as ideas, just as the grin of a fool shoots out from the entire face, a spirit of idiocy, a burden of not knowing that there is another way. It is the same grin that spreads over John's face, roughened in the firelight, sometimes haloed in the starlight, blundering downward, earthward, in a descent that ends and begins with my body.

The next morning when I woke before the rest of them and fought off the throbbing insult of the booze, I was sitting next to him in the passenger seat on the way to the Gas-n-Go. There are bursts of light that shoot from the heads of geniuses, as visual evidence for profound thoughts. The mind and all its thunder, the electric shock of a hot piston-thrilling engine. What else to cool such storms? He went on. The idea, Jenny, is that an intellectual nimbus crowns the heads of clear and bright thinkers. Forehead maybe, or somewhere near the ears.

I turned away and watched the undergrowth and trees pass by outside the window. It might be true that no one really listens to the river, that no one can recite the contours of its murmuring.

I have heard stories about how, in the early days of photography, a considerable amount of hope was placed in the medium's chemical ability to detect spirits. The camera was put to work to capture auras and apparitions of all sorts. After periods of war especially, many families who had lost their sons on the battlefield sought out spirit photographers for one last look. To see where precisely the fatal wound was, or maybe to determine the precise cause of death. What could possibly be gained, even if the loss was accompanied by one last look? These grieving families would say to themselves something like the meagerness of the eyes, the toilsome mortal coil, this delicate tabernacle, this world we live in bondage to, *in* but not *of* is the idea.

And they'd give further voice to their appeals to whatever snake charmer or celestial angler might be at that moment waiting to receive whatever's left of the body once it's been emptied of its person. Those scavengers would take eyes if sight were all we were made of, mouth if voice, teeth if bite. The belief was that the dead are more than thoughts, and maybe thought could have material existence in the new chemical of photography that translated verbatim the unintelligible current of space into a flat image, a provision only a disinterested chemical could supply.

But could it evidence the visible fountain of thought that sometimes flowed from the brow? Or somewhere around the ears, where the chicken hawk does his thinking? John was still talking. Not even a bit, Evenene, since we do not, I shit you not, need now and never have needed a picture of it, need no camera for the pristine business of laying the body down. We've got proof of the fountain right here, and he opened his mouth as though he was going to speak, but the wave of sound stopped, and I took up the question myself.

I opened my mouth as he had and another greater silence swallowed up the sound of the Firebird's rumbling engine, of the sound of the wind rushing in through the passenger side window, the music streaming from the car speaker.

Antistrophic Choral Interlude: She's Got You

There is an old bridge I know of over an obscure part of the Hiwassee River that very few people have seen. Let us close our eyes, inch toward its edge and gaze down into the rushing water below. Let us be afraid neither of the depths nor of the surface. For the surface of the water tells us of its depths only when it is broken. And to break it we must leave the solid ground which the old bridge incarnates, breach that threshold, and submerge ourselves entirely in that virulent substance that rushes toward its own end.

While in the air we close our eyes and breathe in, closing up the bodily routes through which air usually escapes. A part of the extra-aqueous world is taken down into the subaqueous depths with us, stored in the body, but, ultimately, returning to its place of origin above the water, in the warm breeze beside the bank of the river, where we bask in the sunlight and cool the tongue with whatever intoxicating drink we might have beside us.

But the depths, once having been discovered, call to us with a voice that is both our own and not our own. The experience that voice invokes is formed by recognizable contours, but the lilt of the melody and the savor of the rhythm that carries it over those contours are relentlessly otherworldly. And so we take our sweet time, finish the cold beer in hand, relish the last few drags of the cigarette before tossing it off into the dewy grass, and watch the sun lift from the torso and forearm the beads of water that echo faintly the initial inscription of the song of the river upon the body, watching them vanish into thin air as they return to the heavens where the buzzards rule with their own unspeakable thirsts.

We take our time because the progression of the river is timeless and because we know that soon we will be diving back in. For the world is already a lonely place and bridges its loneliest testaments, and so I invite you to dive in with me, here at the edge of this rickety bridge that perhaps no other pair of human eyes has ever set themselves upon.

Down there we will find again another configuration of the voice of the river as it shifts and opens up to make room for the weighty human bodies which we carry along. The multitude of fluvial voices fall silent for a moment and a new voice is formed around our bodies, as a momentary cradle, as a bit of photographic information slurring into memory somewhere behind the eyes. This new opening breaks into song, and we recognize it as the voice of Patsy Cline:

> I've got the picture
> that you gave to me.
> And it's signed with love,
> just like it used to be.

We listen to her inter the heartbreak with our inner ear, but also hear with our skin. For the water that we swim in is no longer a mere medium for the voice but is that voice itself, burying us like a dead memory, but by virtue of that burial, serving the duty of restoration of something lost to recollection itself. We all know that it is impossible to open up the gifts of memory from out of the folds of the past, unless those gifts are no longer in our possession. As we do this, we find it expedient to close our eyes again, in acquiescence to a reflection of the initial dive. The deprivation of underwater sight can increase our sensitivity to the shift in Ms. Cline's voice, up the scale, as she sings the next lines:

> The only thing different;
> the only thing new:
> I've got the picture;
> she's got you.

In closing our eyes not only do we heighten the awareness of the voice, but we also, more importantly, rid ourselves of the body, for a disembodied voice like Ms. Cline's demands a disembodied listener.

What, then, happens to the body? What is its fate here beneath the surface? It is carried along by the currents which now possess it, having become, like the record, the ring, the picture in the song, the concurrence of memory and lost substance. Its initial weight ascribed to us at birth has become a figurative weight that only our feeling for the past can bear:

> I've got your memory—
> Or has it got me?

Let us make a memory not only something a person can have, but also something that can exist outside of the mind that remembers—a disembodied memory which becomes autonomous and which is rewarded agency by the person in whom it was generated. For this is what it means for the memory to have its bearer.

How then can the shock of this possession be overcome? If we breathe and reassert the priority of the body, then the voice that envelops us will release us from its grip and, having regained the life contained in the body, we will at the same time be losing it, for we are, remember, under water. Nor will it work to merely throw away the picture, the records, the class ring. These activities are ill-advised because they miss the point: it is the memory as a roving abstraction that precedes these objects and will therefore survive even if they are discarded.

From time to time we find ourselves tricked into deep thinking. If lucky, we will recognize the trick and stop before diving down into unknown regions and will save ourselves from looking too deeply into things, for that habit leads to discomfort because in the end we'll always see more than we had originally wanted to see. It is better to swim ourselves back into the shallows, and content ourselves with what we see on the surface of the water, which holds no intimation about how far down the water might go. There is of course the old saying that swift-moving water implies shallows, and slow-moving water implies great depths. But, as we all know from the tragedy of the Evenene girl last summer in our Hiwassee, this adage has serious limitations.

Although the contents of the memory are located in the past, the memory itself is oriented to the present. It is the tactile fluidity of the present that provokes the song into existence. The song's possession, however, of our disembodied voice doubles in the form of the minutiae that recalls the intimacy of complete submersion:

I've got the picture
that you gave to me,
and it's signed with love,
just like it used to be.
The only thing different,
the only thing new:
I've got your picture;
she's got you.

I've got the records
that we used to share
and they still sound the same
as when you were here.
The only thing different,
the only thing new:
I've got the records:
she's got you.

I've got your memory—
Or has it got me?
I really don't know,
but I know it won't let me be.

I've got your class ring
that proves you cared,
and it still looks the same
as when you gave it, dear.
The only thing different,
the only thing new:
I've got these little things;
she's got you.

And so we struggle against it, as a drowning girl struggles against the current. We come up from the water once the song has reached its end; the memory evoked by the voice does not merely cling to the objects around the singer's bedroom, but has become an entity unto itself, an apparition, exerting a harmful influence over the doomed singer. But reconciliation is found in the lingering beads of water spilled from the body that has now reclaimed its native ground, precipitate and luminous in the sunlight of whatever side of the river we might have ended up on, just as the memory of the melody itself glides through time and thereby becomes an impermanent testament to the temporal flux that began long before we leapt from the bridge. For the moment a song is begun is the moment we can anticipate its end. Though the saddening memory might hold sway over both listener and singer for a little while, we are comforted in knowing that this sway is contingent upon a life that is ultimately brief, disembodied and hollow.

Whatever was on the other side of the mountain was a veil more heavy than the darkness just beyond the headlights that masks our speed as we drive down the highway each night, emptying the world of distinction by sheer acceleration, closing in on the center by retreating from the center, renouncing distance mile by mile, hour by hour, breath by breath. The mountain was both near and impossibly far.

And there was Nathaniel on his side of the river. When he drinks his body takes in not just the booze but also the air, the rich contours of the sounds that hang near the river, and the way his eyes take in the sights of the river. The animals do not hide from the clamor of his human eyes. They creep around him, keeping their distance, but never disappear completely.

When I wake the next morning sometimes I take with me a few beers down the path to the river, and I try to keep pace with him, tossing to the side the empty cans, ignoring the pulsing blood in my head and the inertia of my hands, as I open another and take a long pull, tipping my head back as he does, releasing the air that has been held during the long pull, parting the grass with my hand as I focus on the figure there on the other side. I try to see if I can detect the precise moment at which the alcohol hits my mind, then eyes, and steadies me for another drink, a harder one since there on the other side of the water the next drink Nathaniel takes is also harder, and more satisfying, more troubling to that vacant magnitude of thirst. He kills it as I kill it as we all kill it, but he holds what's been killed differently.

And John takes the mountain, too. He takes it as a suggestion that the world might be able to move with the body, both finding something to spurn.

After I woke the next morning, it was late morning again and we were driving to the gas station. I was in the passenger seat and John talked about his Firebird. The engine, Jenny, is a separate entity, engine and car often being counterposed in all likely physical applications. Each has its own desires, its own body, its own demise. The body is the dead shell, and the paneled exterior is a painted corpse. The engine is the voice of the car, and comprises the body's defense, when the mechanical chain of events moves from the driver's mind to his foot, to the gas pedal and on from there. The driver deceives himself if he thinks he possesses the car, deceives himself, too, if he thinks this car cares one bit about his safety, or the safety of his girl riding shotgun.

He hit the steering wheel for emphasis. You see, Evenene? This thing don't feel. There's the sound of fingernails scratching the surface. What is the surface but a noise haunting our hands?

There was the sound of the wind coming into the car. I closed my eyes and listened. The exterior is nothing was what John was saying. It only cuts us off from the car's truest desire for speed. He told me to roll down my window. I rolled down the window and put my arm out into the late-summer air. It was hot outside. I could sense the river, close by, even though it lay beyond the thick foliage that streamed past us. I looked out the window at the passing trees and tried to see the opening where the river would be.

You see, Jenny, that's too much for us and our frail bodies. Too much for the brain and senses when it blasts our eyes. The wind smells different at these speeds. Confuses the senses.

I brought my arm back into the car and rolled up the window. The engine, though, the engine understands and thirsts after speed. At least a good one does. Again he hit the steering wheel. Nothing, he said. Then he pressed the gas pedal, and the car shook a bit as it picked up speed. You see that. You hear that. It's not just the heartbeat but the living being inside, like the soul. It is the reason for being. The car is just the weight. The perfect car would not even have seats. It would not invite passengers and would not need a driver. Would just go because going is what it was meant to do.

He was still accelerating. The brush along the highway looked like a single streaming mass, and the road blasted by in uniform measure. And these painted yellow lines, he said, pointing out over the steering wheel, these are the food the car eats, the miles are eaten up by a good engine, and spit back out like bones or teeth. That's what those lines are there for—they're the regalia of fishbone holding the asphalt flesh of highway together, keeping cars from smashing into one another, yes, ostensibly, but they serve a more sinister purpose—sucking the life out of all speed and force and momentum—food for the powers of horses and gasket. The body, its burdensome chassis and shiny panels, hates the engine and the engine hates the body, even though they both need each other.

We were turning a curve and I felt the car slow down.

Reggie had wandered off somewhere and left the gas nozzle in the tank of the Firebird. The trigger was still down, and the hose shook back and forth on the ground as it delivered fuel to the car. The valve clicked and the mechanism within halted the flow of gas. I gripped the handle, shook the nozzle, and removed it, slowly, watching that strange, almost weightless substance, perpetually ready to ignite, fall from the tip as I balanced it back onto the pump. A few drops fell to the asphalt, and vanished into the air.

The sunlight spread over the windshield of the car, and the glare steadied me against the dizziness caused by the fumes. Then

John came out of the fueling station loaded up with a couple of cases of beer, cradling in his arm a paper sack, smiling with an unlit cigarette between his lips. He heaved one case onto the roof of the car, balanced the paper bag on his knee and swung the door open with this free hand. He presented me with a beer, unopened, sweating, then loaded up the provisions and parked the car a ways off in the parking lot of the gas station, far enough away from the tanks to smoke the cigarettes he'd just obtained.

He turned off the engine and got out. I could hear the radio faintly streaming from the speakers. We stood for a moment drinking and said nothing. He took my hand, then my waist, and propped me onto the hood of the car, where we lay with our backs against the windshield and stared up at the treeline beyond the highway. He was content, one hand on his car, the other on his drink, having placed all bodily trust in whatever was before him, without question, satisfied simply because that was what was there, and not something else.

The aroma of gasoline still hung faintly in the air, but it faded as the time passed and we got more drunk. The music was too low for me to make out the words. A little ways off to my right, near the gas pumps, Reggie sat on his wood leg stool, and beyond him, in the distance, was Nathaniel, watching Reggie, serene, leaning against an enormous oak tree. He hummed to the quiet of the afternoon, and we drank to the quiet of the engine in its repose. We closed our eyes together and sank further into the daylight as the morning stretched into afternoon.

I shifted my weight there on the car and the whole hulking mass shifted, too. Then John jumped down off the hood to get another beer. Deep inside the car, I could hear the fuel splashing softly against the walls of the gas tank where it was stored, ready for the road. Between the trees in the distance, there was the highway enjoying the black esteem of distance. Its fortune is collapse, John says, its composure the work of federal code, to whose enforcers the road is a lavish and obscene trench where commerce can ebb and flow.

In a few hours, we would be there at the road again, astonished upon its streamlined form. That form, John says, is borrowed from the emetic gorge that traces the circular duration of life, and the asphalt tarmac—the gravel and labor that goes into traversing the individuated points, running roughshod through the vector of a bacterium, spinning out its productive silk like the worm at the heart of theologic planks, binding fuel to the road the same way a venereal blush binds two lovers. The tires cling to the road, Jenny, the same way the driver must keep his hands on the wheel if he wants to get to where he's going safely, strikingly, apodictically, and not be vexed by the filth that demands the feet move forward, the eyes move forward, the heart move forward.

Chasing liquor down, I'm told, interferes with a job that must be done, because it turns the two sources of the imagination against one another. If I were breathing fire I could wash the liquor down with river water, since the two are elementally opposed. One draws half of me along the worn path edged with rich ivy and sapling to the bank of the river, and the other toward the leaping flames of the blaze at the center of the camp at night that mimics the spark of life, as it quickens the shadows of the beech trees and oaks that form the boundary of the woods here.

That is like saying day and night have equal share in this place. They have joined without losing their whatever it is that makes them distinct from one another. I look to the east and see a single moment. I look to the west and see the same single moment. I dig into the ground and find time buried there, in the motionless surrender of the soil, the way the kids here dig into the ash to find the flame.

The earth enters my body through the fingertips, and my hands are caked with its mulching singularity, crumbling, moist, fertile, and luminously black. John sometimes says that the most delicate part of surveying the ash of human history, and the parallel histories of thirst and vision, is being able to keep straight the number of bodies each has claimed.

Beside the river bank, I dig and dig into the earth, raising it up to my face for inspection. Seeing nothing but another surface, I loosen my grip and let it fall. The marks I make in the earth signify nothing; they are gone each morning, swept away into the valves of the night. Entire ages come into being and pass away in this manner. I see the white ornament of the trumpet creeper open up and announce the destruction that my slender fingers have wrought here in the soil, and I dig further and further into the ground with the river as my witness and the incipient nations crawling like ants up out of the wound that I am inflicting here.

I once heard that there was an old god before me, his feathered body strapped with dynamite and bearing the weight of the head of a buzzard who grew lonely and created the world long ago by massaging it into a great telluric globe. The story goes that his shadow watched him as he worked the earth through his talons. Looking on, his shadow interrogated him about his intentions. For the shadow coveted his sole companionship with the dark feathers of the bird, with the darkness of the primal ocean waters that were the only substance of the world at that time.

But the great divine buzzard ignored this sinister interlocutor by ridding himself of his ears, which is why, the story says, the buzzard now is deaf. Once he was satisfied with what he had fashioned from the earth, and having silenced his shadow, he hurled the ball of clay and soil into the river and it formed land. Initially, this land was slicked over with birthing fluids, and the only creatures that could thrive there were those repulsive insects and beasts of the swamp. These creatures mated and their progeny were misshapen, oviform, tentacled monsters that writhed and slid along and fed off the flesh of mosquitoes that swarmed above. But this divine buzzard spread its great wings and dried the earth that he had launched into existence, and as the fluids dried, man crawled out of his dark underground dwellings to enjoy the sunlight.

Of destinations in general, he continued, there is a single paved condition of the reticula that completes the daily circuit, and it begins with the hand of labor, crosses that gate of the mouth, and enters triumphant into the body predestined as waste. I agree with him that there is no endpoint that has not been ripped from the foul predicament of our own bodily putrefaction.

John opened his eyes and leaned forward there on the hood of the car where we sat. Imagine on this road before us, Jenny, an appraisal of human life that seeks to justify the beginning middle and end of mankind by enumerating the steps as they dance the dance of all four cardinal directions. And imagine the entire automotive world clinging to this single hope, that their steps will coincide upon some surface the earth has not yet learned the name of. Though this is no reason to get discouraged, because it takes steady hands to strike down whatever distance might persist between the present point and the destination. No one has steady hands, and so we make machines to steady our hands and complete the tasks our various tremblings forbid. What neither hand nor machine knows is what we learn there on the road, when the individuated parts fail to find illumination and the whole thing becomes a solid black mass to penetrate at gorgeous speeds, and we become initiated into this secret according to which, Evenene, there is no higher achievement than striking distance in accord with those tremors diffused over countless nights underneath the bones in our bodies, and countless parts underneath the hood of this car, behind the console, and through the elegant underbelly of the automobile, and choosing this violence with the will or against the will, frivolously, stupidly, the gruesome falling away of the miles, hurled into the darkness on both sides of the road.

He was fully reclined now on the windshield, drunk and gazing up at the mountain to the east. I thought of the great buzzard that had stretched out its wings and carried him up to the very place he would never go, the very place that demanded too much of him in its demand to be seen. The mountain seemed to stare down at us, flaunting the blunt truths it held. John always says that things that hold no secrets are intolerable.

It wasn't the sky we were looking up into. John had his eyes closed still, and kept them closed when he brought his beer to his lips. The music from the radio receded further into the distance, more like an echo keeping time than an actual presence moving over and through the physical contours of the car. I heard it once said that the waves of sorrow or joy a person feels when listening to music come from the momentum of the ether of the spinning earth colliding with the physical substance of the song, and that the subsequent debris of this collision is what influences a person under the sway of its auditory current, so that a moving song is really the bits of the world moving through a listener.

I watched the sky. There was nothing in it to stifle the bodily song the drink had begun to sing in me. And there was nothing there to trouble the perpetual motion that we share with the animals. Their eyes are dim with the morning light and issue out at night the necessary dissolution of the effects of daylight in a flash of the night's collapsed and vital wholeness, without any effort, without a second thought about the flat and abstract planes which we impose upon them. These are two sides of the same flux, indistinguishable from one another, each a totality independent of the other, forged without tools, consumed without swallowing.

Imagine, Jenny, he said, stepping out into a clearing beside the river and seeing a deer there taking a step backward or forward, in near piss impossibility, since backwards and forwards are coupled only to the human tongue, were born there and will die there, just as the east and the west were once gathered from the same river, as two stones plucked up just like that out of a clear stream, plucked up by the human tongue and lodged into place for a brief time. The distinction will fall away when the highway gives up its final secret and the brush bursts forth to reclaim the road.

He drained the last of his beer and looked to the east. That mountain there—if it's a pulse it's got, then we can outrun it, wait it out down here, curse up and down the road while that pulse quits its body and surrenders its words to the void. That mountain there—that is where I slew the great buzzard with a single, innocent yawn, and drank his blood. Do you know from what part of his bird body I extracted the blood? It was the eyes. The buzzard sees all the plains to the west of here, the fence lines, where the animals go to die when the open field has become too much of a burden, when hiding becomes the same thing as running. I sucked the eyes out of that fucking buzzard. They were the size of steering wheels. You see, the bird can see everything and all his best blood is stored there. Having taken in so much with the eyes, the world is there, transformed into some crimson reservoir of decay. It was the richest and filthiest stuff I'd ever dreamed.

KEEGAN JENNINGS GOODMAN

Three

ASHES TO ENGINE, DUST TO DUST

The eyes of the congregation could be saying that hell is on the heel. It is the shadow of the river—not the river itself—that is inscribed there below the brow, as it is the voice of the river that slithers from their mouths, a demonic injunction, harmonies reversed, confused, garbled, barbed, and black.

Here in this valley there are few other sounds that pierce the veil of quietude that has fallen over us. We drive, pressing on, stopping at times, and at other times, passing by, here taking a piss break, there refueling at the gas station, shooting past roadside signs, gravel, dry ditch, wet ditch, broken bottles, all clamoring for attention. Sometimes we pull off the shoulder to wander through the woods or open fields.

John's eyes change when he examines the distance, and so he keeps them close to the ground. There, he said, squawroot. He was pointing to an umbrous, conical plant at the foot of a beech tree. There, Jenny, the parasitic plant spurns the sunlight, and in that refusal seeks a more sinister source, the source of shadow and spite. At what point does its pulse quicken? I walked over and knelt beside him, regarded the strange plant. He turned to me and lead me away.

My arm around him, I could feel moisture there, and the soft flesh made me want to call out for thunder to come and scare us back to camp, scare up the dust, out of thirst, motion, terror and speed, anything that holds the body together, in a single spot, where the luxurious elements of physical being can be cursed. John always says that to be pinned down to a body, even one that can slip inside another with all the greased ease of the knife, to be given breath and a name and a set of eyes to see with and a set of ears to hear with, and fists to clench and thirst to fuel—that to have all of these obscenities performed upon the soul—that all of this is itself a turn of the engine whose inner longings are the only ones worth knowing.

The fragrant afternoon yielded to us, to the body of the car and what it leaves behind. The pace slowed. The drink sank and the blood cowered in its toxic presence.

Far off from the gas station the river murmured. When we pull out of the filling station, the whole valley parts like red water, yielding to our pace, perfected by the engine, determined by a complex puzzle of moving parts, liberating us from the mania of numbers, signs, and specifications.

When we are racing down the black sleeve of the road at night, I lose all awareness of the composite parts of the body of the car and look upon it as a force whose center is aligned with the larger movements of the earth, in the upper regions, in the lower regions, grazing the varied plans of whatever murderer planted asphalt here, a mountain there, whatever river god or frenzied serpent planted a river here, a gas line there, whatever mystery can claim the favor of the eyes, whatever life might trail away into the weeds growing at the side of the highway, whatever inches are gained, stature accomplished in the air of momentary collision, fracture, breaking pads, whatever was once and forever fooled outward and simplified—all of this must yield to us, and we, in turn, must allow ourselves to be known by the car, taken into its mechanical and weighty field of perception, when night falls, when morning comes, when the dew on the ground slips beneath the feet or onto the tongue, finding a new body with which to hide from the sun, Evenene, because the sun has no say in these matters any longer. Maybe the river has swallowed it. Maybe we ran it over long ago in the sanctuary of the tread of the tires and left it to think road, mite, torque, and terminus.

Each morning, each morning then afternoon, the river then the gas station, each giving up its claim to growth, John says, in stages of development and progression, which is caught up in an immense retreat here in this valley.

The air receives nothing new. It refuses our efforts to breathe in and exhale. Even when I put my hand outside the window as we drive down the highway in the late afternoon, the swift-moving air recognizes it. My hand breaks nothing, interrupts nothing. Sometimes the thought comes to me that my hand—with its profound inertia—completes what the atmosphere here really is but cannot fully be.

The question is, put simply, whether or not we belong here. John thinks we do. Its morbid stillness draws him in. It is a landscape that cannot be disturbed, even by the most audacious, the most spectacular and stupid curse the body might want to realize in any direction, if those cardinal terms of north, south, east, and west have not undergone that same subtle disintegration occurring on the interiors of everything I see around me, except the Firebird maybe, or the copper paths of whiskey contained in the clear glass bottles.

All the promises of destruction and vandalism stored in his grip have found in this place their perfect counterpart. These promises can be enumerated: they correspond to the strange glowing ciphers on the speedometer, and to the rhythms and guitar licks, the vibrations torn from the air of some impossibly far away source, pulled in by the microphone, transformed onto the tape, then sent again into the air, picked up this time by the antennae of the Firebird, and transformed yet again into the words, heartache, and intoxication of the country singer's voice, guitar, piano, drums. Whatever elemental will rages inside his hands is transferred to the steering wheel, transformed through that tactile connection and maddened beneath the hood of the car, where the secret of this place must reside.

The landscape around us never takes a breath. Nor does it take its eyes off us. We move toward the cash register and at the Gas-n-Go without the resistance of poverty, toward the promise of drunkenness we secure, the money we find in our pockets each morning, crisp, odorless, and weightless, and there is no friction in any of it.

I have heard it said that mercy is something that is poured out, and that poor souls bathe in it or drink it up. Over the face of this valley, though, is a suffusion not of blood, nor of mercy, but of soil, and it creeps in through the thoughts, the pores, and is immense in its demand for surrender.

When we left the gas station I waved at Reggie in the side view mirror.

John said that the reason nothing moves here is that we're always moving, always taking it in through our eyes, ears, our lovemaking, into our guts through the mouth, as we swallow down this good American lager, and encase the stillness of the whiskey settling down in our teenage depths, or pulling up the underside of thirst to give it definite shape, form, extension, since that's what thirst needs, Jenny, what it cries out for, somebody it can enter, with which it can forfeit its claim to incorporeality, for only a body can be filled, and that vessel smirks toward some vague sense of a new day. Only emptiness can know thirst. Take the highway, vacant as it might seem. What does it thirst for, Jenny? Does it thirst for the body? Or the body's own vacancy? Would it welcome upon its paved palm a body not yet filled with those fluids—whether blood, gin, or ale—that fulfill the thirsts raging deep within us, those thirsts with which the car itself has imbued us? Or would it rather drink into its pores a body that has transformed its thirst into sight, sound, feeling, into a secure grip of the steering wheel, a resplendent curse on the lips, Jenny, a good healthy lust animating the best parts of the naked body, the tips of the fingers, the small of the back?

He was staring hard at the road now, and the sign for the gas station was no longer visible in the side mirror—just a flat, endless stream.

The next morning I woke before the rest of them, disentangled myself from John, still asleep, and went to the river to wash myself. Then we were on the road again, on the way to the Gas-n-Go, and just as I began to settle into the passenger seat, John slowed the Firebird and pulled off the asphalt onto the grassy shoulder of the highway.

He got out of the car and came around my side to open the passenger side door. He stretched his arms and looked around. I know a place here, he said, and stepped into the thicket of sweetbrier that lined the road. I saw there was a narrow trail that led through the brush. I followed and saw him waiting for me. He turned and led me along the trail, overgrown in places, with thorns clutching at my nightgown.

The brush thinned out and opened up to a clearing rimmed with spruce trees on its far side. He paused in the grass and handed me a beer, watching as I expertly cracked it open and drank it down. We walked on, down a gently sloping incline, toward a grove of spruce, which, from here, seemed to go on forever down the ridge. There was no trail now as we walked among the pines, each cloistered in a rigid stance, each apart from its other, as though drawn inward against the still air. We were still descending, and I knew that if we kept going in this direction, we would end up at the bank of the river, or one of the small creeks that fed into it.

Then the ground leveled out and we were in a wood of beech and oak. There was a canopy of leaves overhead, obscuring the light already diffused by a thick layer of cloud above. It seemed as though dusk had suddenly descended upon us, or we upon it, as though the hours had been lost in our own downward climb. A lone crow cried out above us, and I traced the arc of his path as the shrill cry grew fainter.

We walked more slowly now, side by side through the wood. We stopped and John surveyed the area before us. Through a thick patch of scrub oak I caught sight of another clearing, and I thought I heard the sound of flowing water. John led me on, through the oak to the clearing of tall wild grass and creepers climbing up a line of old worn stones, the remnants of a wall or old foundation, he said as we stepped over them.

To my right, I saw another indication of a wall, thickly overgrown and barely visible, then another up ahead. It's an old graveyard, he said, and now I saw the cracked and lichened gray stones jutting from the ground at all different angles. I went up to one and parted the wild grass that obscured it. There was an inscription, but it all shifted the moment my eyes tried to take it in and the lines remained unintelligible to me, effaced not by wind or rain or time, but by the mere act of trying to decipher its engraved meaning.

This is all a floodplain, he said, presenting it to me with a great sweep of his arm. The river is just beyond those trees, over there, and in the spring the waters cover all of this, come to drown the dead they'd already long ago taken away.

Strophic Choral Interlude: Automotive Elegy

Early last Sunday morning, as the late night crowd still held fast in the embers of weekend carousing, their activities having not stopped to recognize the calendar's officious snap into place at midnight, these motivated by and in turn further motivating amorous tremors and stupid grins, whistle-baits, sour-mesh vows and malty curses, early at an hour when the swing was in full, as it has been said, and the night a vintage blue, an automobile of extraordinary allure and appearance broke down in front of a traffic light on Third and Reaves Street. The responsibility to inform the Graysville public of this car has fallen most solemnly upon me.

It was a Dodge Charger with an unremarkable V6, busted windshield wipers, twin exhaust pipes possessive of the tendency to foul up the air in their wake, a leather interior, and a few dents on the rear chrome bumper. None of which contributed whatsoever to the Charger's local fame.

No, the Charger was famous for its paint job. The owner, whose name shall remain withheld, had been struck with the idea—not a great one by any measure—to paint on the body of the car airbrushed portraits of every girl who'd fallen under his spell and completed that fall in the back seat of the Charger. We can all see how this decision could deter potential passengers and serve as a distinctive mark of opprobrium in the eyes of vigilant parents. But it would be too easy to dismiss that auto's veneer as the adolescent braggadocio of some small-town sprout fancying himself a Casanova.

What first comes to our attention is that there simply are not that many girls painted on the car. The artist—for having seen the car first-hand, I have no reluctance in calling him that—was not one to impress by inflated numbers. As it is not my intention to belittle the man's accomplishment, nor aggrandize it, I shall limit my remarks about the number of portraits by stating that there were no more than ten and no less than eight.

Gazing at the women inhabiting unlikely corners of the car's exterior, it might be reasonable to assume the formal appearance of the portraits should vary according to pre-arranged concepts, to infer something about the nature of the backseat relations from the stylistic idiosyncrasies, the relative scale and coloration of the images. We find them near the headlights, on the sides of the doors, on the trunk. Each possesses an individuating feature—a gesturing hand swept across the forehead, a glint in the eyes, an impressionistic stroke of improbable hue. But there is little in the way of psychological insight regarding the youthful misadventures. No, the portraits, although not masks themselves, effectively mask the motivating feelings of the driver of the Charger.

This is not to imply that the images lacked emotion. Take for instance the girl just above the front right wheel well, a blond-haired youth of no more than sixteen, her eyes fixed upon the viewer, her hair a golden pyramid behind her, rippling in motion with the passing air. She is at home at such breakneck speeds as the Charger enjoys. But there is a subtle turn of the upper lip, that look someone gets the moment a disconcerting scent is detected. Directly below her is the right-front tire, its tread worn thin, its repetitious turning perhaps a sign to the girl that for the whole to get anywhere at all, some of its parts have to do a lot of spinning in circles.

The most striking painting is that which emblazons the hood of the Charger. On most cars, this plane is left vacant, to emphasize the power which it contains underhood. There is something reticent about the woman depicted there. Her thick lips are parted, the suggestion of the tip of the tongue, gleaming near the teeth, too wet and lovely to be vindictive, but capable of capping the engine's rhapsodies.

Now, in an automobile we speak of torque. It is neither moment, momentum, nor speed but the rotational counterpart of force. Its equation, then, is: $t = r(F)$, where r is the particle's position vector relative to the fulcrum and F is the force acting on the particle. There are many ways of measuring it, pound-force-feet, or foot-pounds-force, or inch-pounds-force or, for smaller occasions, ounce-force-inches or, in European contexts, meter-kilograms-force (also known as the kilogram-meter). But the official unit is the Newton-meter (N_m) and is expressed as: $E = tq$, where E is energy, t is torque and q is angle moved, in radians.

Torque is, arguably, a discreet measurement. It does not often come under the scrutiny of the driver, is not put on ostentatious display as speed or horsepower might be, is not often boasted. These airbrushed paintings, one could say, possess for the famed Charger as well as for the viewer a kind of torque. The moment of love—no matter how clouded by liquor or teenage myopia, no matter how soured by those awkward moments which so often deny the youthful lover the concomitant post-coital bliss enjoyed by more seasoned couples—that moment of love fueled by all the wrong motives, so often slapstick, so often cruel, keeps us spinning with an invisible force, and if our spiritual machinery is in place, all bearings greased, all belts healthy, all spark plugs charged, all stems, arms, and axles aligned, then we might just be able to make those miles of loneliness disappear. With the help of the rough circuitry of entangled bodies, we may bring ourselves the fleeting pleasures that belong to such tight spots as the backseat of a car.

But in the end, the car breaks down. Certainly, this is the end of the line for that illustrious Charger. It'll take up residence upon a cinder block pedestal, remain on display there in the front yard of its owner. Never again will its seats receive the baptismal spume of upturned bottles of Budweiser. Never again will the interior fill with marijuana smoke or hear the minor ecstasies of minor and momentary champions. Never again will that car slide along underneath the streetlamps' estranging shock-electric blue some late and rainy springtime Saturday night. Never again will its door open to a young local girl assuming the stance of the intrepid heroine braving the waters so often descried in cautionary country songs. We leave it up to her to wonder whether or not it was all futile, just as we must leave unanswered the meaning of the images there on the hood of the Charger, and instead praise girl and car and painterly hand alike for the unlikely and unhappy accomplishments of youth.

We pulled out of the gas station and this time I failed to wave at Reggie in the rearview mirror. The windows were down, and as the car picked up speed I watched the mountain, solitary and gray, loom in the horizon in the side mirror.

Everything around us—the tangle of undergrowth, the overhanging branches, roadside weeds and bracken, all the bright litter along the side of the highway, the trees beyond it, the opaque screen of the woods, and the overcast sky—seemed to have enacted that last gasp of surrender long ago. The road did not lead to the mountain. Nor did the road lead away from it. The distanceless hours we drove on that highway never escaped its shadow. And if night was an extension of the mountain's shadow, then it swallowed us with a slow kind of certainty.

But it was daylight now, and my head was dizzy with it. As the origin of the river, the mountain, whether blazing or blind, pushes blood up to the front of the eyes, just as it pushes water and whiskey through the rocky veins and ravines. We were on the road, and the afternoon light began to change, dressed now in a new hour.

John's congregation caravanned alongside us. As each vehicle passed by, I could see its driver, staring ahead the same way they stare at night into the fire, with a narcotic indifference to the fury John raises with his attempts to give expression to the holy suffering of his Firebird. I kept my eyes on the mountain, even though I always had the feeling that looking at it demanded more than the feeble power of sight. If the river is its voice, and the clouds its thoughts, then it has only ever had one thing to say, and that means it speaks a final word and a first word in the same stony breath.

The next morning I woke and made my way down to the bank of the river. My mouth was dry. I cupped my hands and drank, feeling the water rush around my tongue, my teeth, the back of my throat.

There was a story I heard once about the human voice and how it first blossomed over the surface of the earth. The story tells of two boys walking through the forest, one good and the other evil. Both were approaching manhood. They had come to a clearing, a great field of goldenrod. As they crossed the field they were startled by the sight of a beautiful woman who lay in their path, shivering naked in the tall grass. A heavy rope around her neck bound her hands and feet together.

Now in these days, the story goes, it was the animals alone who knew how to speak, mankind not yet having learned this art. The evil boy therefore did not know he was evil, and the good one did not know he was good. Upon seeing this woman, the evil child began to kick and pummel her. He bruised her ribs, tore her hair, and bloodied her mouth. He ravaged and violated her within the limits of his imagination, spending the measure of his youthful energy in this way. Fatigued, he collapsed on the grass beside the beaten woman and fell asleep.

The other child, being good, ministered to the poor woman's wounds. He covered her shivering body with his own coat, wiped the blood from her mouth and eyes, and consoled her with gentle caresses. As night fell, he, too, fell asleep beside the woman.

The children woke the next morning, and their divergent passions were renewed and intensified by the bright sunlight and the sound of benevolent and rapacious animals all around. The evil child resumed his torment upon the body of the bound woman, and, when spent, fell exhausted and satisfied once again in the tall soft grass. The good child resumed, too, his ministrations and nursed the wounds of the woman, offering her the meager comfort he could against the pain the evil child had inflicted. And so it went on like this for many days. Each morning the children woke with renewed stores of energy and inspiration, seeing the work before them which they would realize upon the body of this woman, the one for evil, the other for good.

One night a strange sound broke the silence of the peaceful field, luring the boys from their sleep. They sat up and listened. The woman had heard it, too, for her swollen eyes were open and held a look of alarm. The sound came again, from the east. It was a long, drawn-out cry, dropping off finally into a whimper, only to rise again to a new height of panic. Each boy looked at the other and they rushed off together to retrieve what could only be, they knew, an anguished animal. They followed the sound and happened upon a young fawn, who had been mortally wounded and was now struggling to run on legs that no longer could carry it.

The two boys seized the creature, dragged it into the field and dropped it near the woman. Each hoped for his own reason that she would learn the song of the dying animal, and that they might hear this song come from her lips. The evil child abused the woman, until he grew tired, and the good child likewise consoled her. Instead of falling asleep as they had before, they waited long into the night and listened to the animal's cries. There was nothing of the fear of death in this cry. Nor protest against a life cut short. There was nothing meditative whatsoever in the death chant of the deer. It came from an immediate distress, yet a distress that never quite broke into sheer panic. The only clear impression the deer's cry gave was that of isolation. For the deer was not calling out to them. Nor was it calling out to an approaching void. It was calling out in mournful accord with the same force that makes the wind moan. And so the boys were lulled asleep by the song, first the evil one, then the good one.

The voice of the deer dropped off to a mere whimper. There was fluid gathering in the lungs of the creature now, and it did not have long to live.

The woman stared vacantly in its direction. It beheld her and understood that her end was going to be a bad one. The creature then opened its mouth as wide as it could to invite her in. She immediately understood and began crawling, hands and feet still bound, over the soft grass toward the animal, whose open mouth widened in welcome. The woman crawled into it, her hands and ankles still bound, and hid there inside the body of the creature.

Morning came with the songs of birds and dew drops heavy at the ends of the blades of grass. When the evil child awoke to resume his labors upon her body, he found that she had vanished. The good child woke, too, and looked around with wonder and disappointment. Only the deer was there, dead now. Both children were enraged and saddened by their loss.

They each procured a knife and began to butcher the deer, fiercely hacking away at it until they heard a sound like no other they had ever before heard. It startled them and caused them to hack away more violently at the deer, ripping its meat, breaking bone, ligament, tendon, gristle, but the sound grew more shrill and more intense, and the boys grew more frightened, more frenzied with their knives. The sound crescendoed, then began to drop off, before becoming a gurgling whimper. Then the whimpering lost its sense of desperation and became simple, brutish noises, irregular, labored, fainter and fainter. The boys' knives slowed, too. They could see clearly now that it was the woman's body. Her flesh had mixed with that of the deer, her blood with its blood, and now, its voice with her voice.

We moved through the world. The world did not move through us. We drove off from the gas station and pulled onto the highway in the Firebird. I drank, put my hand out the window and felt nothing. John drank and tore speed from the asphalt. The sound of the revolving engine unburdened me. The image of the road faded from my eyes. In its place emerged the same void I would meet at night, every night before the next morning when I woke and walked down to the riverside to wash the taste of sleep from my mouth and watch Nathaniel drink, swim, and gather sticks on the other side of the river.

John shifted in the driver seat and without taking his eyes off the road reached into the back seat and grabbed another beer, opening it in a single fluid motion as he brought it up to his lips and swallowed it down. The evening was approaching. I could sense it in the dull collaboration of light and stillness lingering on the leafy boughs of the trees on the side of the highway.

We both settled into the speed we had acquired in the car. The motion was direct, definitive, and soothing. John remained silent, drinking himself down the road. Often, I look to the right, then to the left, east back toward the mountain, then west out over the river basin, with splinters of some vague hope scattered before me on the shifting horizon.

I have heard of people who ignite old worn-out tires with a fiery speech, people who bring down fences with a call to a lover trapped on the other side, people who can empty a whiskey glass with a mere gleam of the eye. It is the unreadable texture of youth that makes them believe they can do it.

John says that we are given over to the false hope of small change rattling in a glass jar. The speed of an automobile, the resistance of the chassis and paneling, the assertions of an axle and its inexorable forward motion as it roars through the void are all the shadowy efforts of the speaker who believes himself capable of trusting his own words. We strike our words like two flints against one another for this very reason. We pluck them from the still air in which they float as invisible jewels on whirling clouds of exhaust.

The appeal of a headstone is its irrefutable uprightness, he says. It is a sign of good alignment outlasting the body careening before fate. It is a sign of our grip on the steering wheel, evidence that each mile gained is another brilliant day in a life worth its weight in paper money. The stones we chisel away at eventually do acquire language—standing upright in the ground, they name the dead. Some say to hell with them, but I want to say no, maybe not, let me take another look. No one can stumble across some Dodge Charger, some V8 Ford pickup, or some long black Lincoln standing upright in the ground and fail to think it a sign of things to come.

The hood scoop is no open mouth. Nor is it an open eye reflecting the blackness that presses down against the blacktop. The hood scoop is a closed mouth and a closed eye, and with it we can prove that the road, the liquor, and the night can be taken blindly, that the two of us can be thrown onto the road and immersed in a forward thrust which, although terrifying, is not so treacherous that it cannot be taken in with a single shut eye. The hood scoop is a revelation that interrupts the still black air pressing against the blacktop, John said.

One night I heard him address his audience sitting scattered throughout the camp, drinking. He said that the phoenix on the hood of the car is ever-ascending from the ashes of a contradiction still smoldering beneath the hood. He told them that the engine makes certain mechanical facts concrete: seven and a half liters, super-duty high output V8, three hundred horse-power, four-hundred and ten pounds per foot net in torque, the heavy counterweight to every cylinder; the crank throw is neutralized by this weight and answers to the vertical pistons in the crankshaft.

These mechanical certitudes rest beneath the hood as empty assertions. Alone, they add up to a weight that can offer nothing, get nowhere at all, quench no fire or thirst, dislodge from the heart or mouth no fear of the paved and murderous open wound surrounding us. He told them that these mechanical facts will never burn and will forever lay dormant as the world eats away at them, with the teeth of some famished adult, broken by work, infected in the body, starved by the forces of daylight and hourly regimentation, crushed beneath the heap of hour upon hour, those hours being torn from the ground, mined with quartz and coal, those hours pinning the soul to the ground, for nothing more than a cold bed. The mechanical facts of the engine are in general discord with the smooth surface of words. These facts of the engine will never ignite, he said, unless doused with some infernal flammable substance.

In his imagination, I knew, he saw his mute congregation drinking in agreement to the indelible truth of his words and the unquestionable and fiery truth of the collision of booze and steel, fire and moving parts. In his fantasy, these kids would then turn their eyes toward the mountain and curse it, speaking these curses into the mouth of an open bottle, and it would not matter if what they uttered was a collection of living words or the decayed rot of words that had died long ago and lost all semblance to meaning.

Inspiration does not inhabit the tongue, according to John. The tongue is a serpent whose nature dictates its locomotions as well as its smooth locutions. No, the imagination is the part of the human lie that is most attuned with the flames of the campfire, and if there's any way to get rid of that mountain, it's to burn it down.

The next place we stopped after the gas station was the bar. John pulled off the highway and up the long gravel driveway which wound along an exposed treeless ridge and wild flowers that had never been cut. The driveway up to the bar cut along the entire face of a hill that had been blasted flat, long ago, with large chunks of gravel. Other parts had been paved—the path from the parking lot to the back entrance of the tavern, and an area in front where a few canvas chairs and some old wood caskets for tables served as a patio that no one had ever used.

As we rounded the final stretch of the driveway, I saw the place come into view. We pulled into the parking lot, where the usual cars and pickups were parked. John turned the Firebird off and we sat for a few moments in silence. He shoved the door open with his shoulder, came around the front end of the car, then swung open my door.

He took me by the hand and led me around to the far side of the building. There was a large heavy Dumpster and some wooden crates packed full of empty beer bottles. Bolted to the siding, there was an old rusted iron ladder. He grabbed a rung and yanked on it, testing its strength. Then he started climbing it up to the rooftop. I followed him, and when I got to the top, he gave me his hand and pulled me up to the flat surface of the building.

We walked to the edge and took in the view. The valley stretched out before us. The highway was visible from here, snaking along the base of the hill we were now on, then straightening out through an open field before curving sharply again further up. Already, parts of the road were covered in shadow. The road itself looked too narrow for us to have travelled it, and too stark a thing to get lost in or on each night before the next morning, when I would wake and find first the cold then my body waiting for me again beneath the blanket we shared there on the ground.

Far off in the distance, the road reappeared and beside it was the river, bounded in by the trees too faint to name, assuming now the first obscurities of shadow that anchor them to the night.

And I followed with my eyes the bends in the river, and the parallel curves in the road, until both seemed to join in the shadows that were stretching themselves low in surrender to the night, which they themselves would join, and my eyes followed the shadow up to the most distant reaches of sight itself, beyond whose limitations only buzzards and paramedics can take us, until my gaze had been redirected by the night in a fluid seamless sweep, back along the contours of the valley, up the highway, the trees and hedgerow, the fields and hollows, all magnified now as though I were drawing them near to me, until I saw my own shadow stretched out before me at my bare feet.

I watched my shadow there move while I remained stationary, and thought of this movement, and how the night draws the shadow into itself, and takes with it the coherence of every extended thing, stealing its unity, unloosing whatever constitutes its most essential core, its soul, from that which has tethered it to its object—the sun—and delivers it as an offering to the sacred night.

And so, the stories go, because the night has received that which the body most dearly possesses, the night grows and has been growing for ages and becomes substance itself. Obscuring in mankind's imagination the distinction between substance and mere quality, it soon acquires an appetite for motion, then self-motion, then love and self-love, and from those, it learns attraction, and from this repulsion, hatred and disgust, and from these it forces open the doors that have been locked to keep it out, and slips into the bedrooms of virgins, whose eyes have not yet learned its name, and confounds the machinations of cops who will never learn that it has swallowed up, too, long ago, both law and all existing order.

And it is only when this divine night has been sated and longs for the sleep of creation does it retreat to the inner core of those bodies that call out for the daylight.

Antistrophic Choral Interlude: Satisfied Mind

After conceding to the beer before us, to the long pull it demands, and its cooling rewards, let us place it gently on the mahogany bar top and consider the faces of the drinkers around us. The bar is filled with solemn shadows. The shadows are the imprecise reproductions of their bearers. So, too, might their faces mask some hidden wisdom or satisfaction held somewhere behind the eyes. They seem to chew their beer, as connoisseurs do. They smoke their cigarettes with a kind of ferocity betrayed in the mouth and in the lungs. Few words are spoken. Laughter is rare. We hear off in the background the collision of billiard balls. We take another drink, and set the bottle down, and we are among them, have become a part of the compositional body that they adhere to, and, if we are paying attention, we may partake of what these patrons of the Matinee know. Sometime over the course of the evening, a song will fill the bar room. It begins with a polyvocal chorus that asks us the following:

> How many times have you heard someone say
> "If I had his money, I could do things my way?"
> Little they know that it's so hard to find
> one rich man in ten with a satisfied mind.

As the song proceeds, the voices that comprise the chorus drop away and a single voice emerges:

> Once I was living in fortune and fame.
> Everything that I dreamed for to get a start in
> life's game.
> Suddenly it happened; I lost every dime,
> but I'm richer by far with a satisfied mind.

The pattern of the individual voice singing out against the backdrop of a collective voice is repeated in the rest of the song:

> Money can't buy back your youth when you're old,
> or a friend when you're lonely, or a love that's
> grown cold.
> The wealthiest person is a pauper at times
> compared to the rich man with a satisfied mind.

And now, again, the single voice continues his narrative:

> When my life is ended, and my time has run out,
> my trials and my loved ones I'll leave them no doubt.
> But one thing's for certain, when it comes my time
> I'll leave this old world with a satisfied mind.

There is a peculiarity of this song that warrants our attention: just what is a "satisfied mind" is never defined. No description of what might be involved in being satisfied is given. Why is this? We might be tempted to believe that a satisfied mind does not need explication because everyone already knows what it is. But this is only a partial answer at best, and a misleading one at worst. For if a satisfied mind varies according to each person, then we could never look to our neighbor, lover, stranger, whomever, for any sort of verification. What satisfies my mind does not satisfy your mind, and what satisfies his mind does not satisfy her mind, and so forth and so on. Yet, on the other hand, if there is some objective criteria for having a satisfied mind, then we should be able to simply say: such and such is what satisfies, so go out into the world and get it. We know it is not money, but it might be something just as hard as cold cash in the hand, just as irrefutable as an unpaid electric bill sitting on the kitchen table. If the latter were the case, then the song's reticence regarding the attainment of satisfaction would make the song nothing more than a cruel tease, its wisdom more like poverty, its affirmation more like denial.

There seems, then, something of an impasse: are we denied an explanation of the satisfied mind because no definition can extend beyond a single individual, or because whatever satisfies every mind is already known with such clarity that it goes without saying? I think neither are the case. And I shall attempt to demonstrate how the impasse is circumvented by the dialogic construction of the song.

The pattern here established resembles call-and-response, but it is more complex. The collective is talking to the single first-person speaker, and, consequently, responding to the narrative information that he discloses. In traditional call-and-response patterns, no alteration occurs: what the caller says is not transformed by the response, and the response is not progenitive—it is merely a response. But in "A Satisfied Mind," the two components make sense only in opposition to one another, and both are changed by the other: there is common wisdom expressed in the first and third verses, but this common knowledge about happiness is derived from the shared experiences the first-person narrator discusses.

The achievement of a satisfied mind must be grounded in the subject's life experience, in his or her own personal failures, losses, triumphs, and wealth. For it is one mind that is either satisfied or not, since single individual satisfaction is a different thing than, say, collective fulfillment. The journey that leads one to conclude, yes, my mind is satisfied is the narrative in play and the details of that story from which we must generalize. This narrative is told in the first-person singular and it is contained in the second and fourth verses. At the end of the song, the singer knows that he will "leave this old world with a satisfied mind." He is certain, but how is this possible? No one has told him how to get a satisfied mind, nor told him what that even entails.

The collective voices in the first and third verses are only telling him what does not lead to satisfaction. More specifically, they are telling him that money is going to do him very little good. It cannot bring back "youth when you're old, or a friend when you're lonely, or a love that's grown cold." This knowledge conforms to a pattern of rhetorical speech, and this pattern is set up from the start of the song: "one rich man in ten" is not just hard to find, though it is certainly that, but more importantly, it is indicative of how infrequently money leads to happiness. The polyvocal wisdom does not contradict what the first-person speaker says; it does not contradict his story, nor does it really add much insight. Nor is it meant to. It is meant, rather, to speak from a different point of view: rhetoric is speech that does not have the same conditions of truth to which narrative modes of speech must subject themselves. This is because rhetoric is distanced from the actual events that make up a story: it is wisdom as an accretion of narrative events, and it is reliable precisely because it is not reducible to the experience of the single individual of whom and to whom it speaks. Thus the assertion that, yes, I have a satisfied mind, makes its appeal to some aggregate possession of human collectivity, and can reside in the individual in a rhetorical and epigrammatic form. For it has an objective status that reveals what it already was, but remained hidden in its origins.

And these origins are the subjective experiences of others who, like the narrator in the second and fourth verses, have gone through life, a person who was perhaps once "winning in fortune and fame," but who suddenly "lost every dime." Such experiences are the sensuous sediment of everyday life—the chewed-on beer, the burning cigarette, the cold harsh wind, or the oppressive heat. And they gather somewhere behind the eyes or between the lines of a country tune, and they have the smell of the burning paycheck, which is also the scent of whiskey, the feel of a sore lower back, which is also the slow narcotic slur of the gin, and the taste of one last round, which is as much a warning against loneliness as it is the promise of an enduring bed. Such experiences belong to the man who, after a few hours at the bar, might stagger outside to the half-empty parking lot out back to careen before the setting sun and listen to the traffic move along the nearby highway, and who, while zipping up his fly, might find himself humming a tune assuring him with its melodious force that when his time has come to leave this old world for what it is and not for what it cannot be, he'll be able to leave it, friend, with a satisfied mind.

Together we finished the last beer, passing it back and forth with no words between us. We stared straight through the windshield into the parking lot of the Matinee. The stillness of dusk had settled over things. The lights were on above the bar. The sign radiated its fluorescent glow but the effect was lost in the smoldering red sky behind it.

When the beer was gone John leaned back in the driver seat and fished through his pockets for the bills and the change he knew would be there. He pulled it all out in a handful, looked at it without counting it, closed his fist and left the car. I watched him walk through the gravel parking lot to the back entrance of the Matinee. He stood waiting until the heavy wood door opened and the figure of Gerome Mainder appeared in the threshold. They shook hands and together disappeared inside the bar.

I thought of Nathaniel, the image of his body broken by drink, but somehow put back together by its collusion with the river and the thousand simultaneous movements, in the trees, upon his face, the fluttering birds at the edge of sight. The air disturbs the mind there, and here the mind disturbs the air.

The eyes of Nathaniel were large and glassy. They reflected both the trouble contained in the bottle and the quietude of the bottle emptied of everything that can be called good. Once after waking the next morning, while sitting on the bank of the river, I watched him slide down into the water. He had removed his clothes with one hand, keeping hold of the brown paper sack that held his liquor, untying his shoes and unbuttoning his pants with his free hand. It was a slow process punctuated by a lot of drinking.

The water that rolled by him also waited for him. He had a six-pack too, and strung it along on the plastic rings in the water. The cans of beer floated nearby as he stood and splashed around. He submerged himself, and appeared moments later, beads of water tumbling down from his head, his long hair clinging to his shoulders, beard glistening in the light. He let the current take him a little ways downstream, then paddled upstream, pausing to drink before paddling some more. He moved as the water moved—without urgency. He emptied in a series of single gulps the cans of beer floating nearby. When the contents were drained, he crushed the can above the water and gave it a shake, as thought to allow the liquid at the bottom of the can to recongregate with the universal stream that flowed around him. Then he turned toward the bank and tossed the can into the brush.

Afterwards he lay in the grass, on his back, staring up at the sky, or into the colors swimming in the black corridors behind his closed eyes. He stretched out, ran his hand over his torso, filled his lungs with the air of his side of the river, drank more.

Only drunks dream of water, John says, and they dream only of water, cannot in fact dream of a figure that is not drenched, sated, sealed, water being a translucence stolen from the perverse heights of the heart, Jenny, water being the foundation for every satisfaction of the flesh and demanding a vigilance of the drinker, so that nothing is poisoned by the needy human tongue breaking the surface in the morning, constituting that surface in the evening, somewhere between buried and resurrected over the course of the vain and invisible drama that marks the transformation of one into the other.

I suppose it is true enough that water dreamed is water set up in opposition to all the creatures, as John says—the deer and her fawn, the hawk and its brood, the hare and its litter. These wakeful things approach the edge of the river and drink their way into harmony with the forces that remain just beyond the reach of any human who tries to heed his duties to love and avoid speaking out of turn. Only the heedless will be able to drink as the animal drinks, without braking for turns, without caring about the next day's tasks, without serving up upon a silver tongue the verities of the fold.

The next morning I woke before the others, slipping out from beneath the blanket that John and I shared, and made my way, barefoot, down the dirt path that lead to the water. Our side of the river was motionless even when John and I moved through it. Nathaniel's side became exaggerated with movement even when he remained still.

Melodies slipped out from between his humming lips. They traveled into the air, fragments of song lost in the water, in the leafy treetops, to the ears of the animals. Other parts remained suspended over the water and made it to our side of the river, where speech and song departed without consequence. His thoughts were eerie melodies blossoming in the morning above him, shelters of sobriety against a storm of drunkenness. They were warnings to the other inhabitants of his side of the river to keep away.

I understood his appetite from afar, understood what time had demanded of his body. The visual assertion of his worn-out body had traveled over the same distances the voice had traveled. Or maybe, I thought, these melodies were in preparation of traveling that distance, moving in the same ethereal channels, preparing a path that insinuated itself into his heart, masked as it was by the toxic portion sliding through his guts.

Then I imagined Nathaniel here among us, on our side of the river. I imagined him sitting around the campfire, taking the smoke into his lungs, giving the dancing light half his attention, even as the mouth shaped the air into words that none of us could know, words that would be washed away by drink. I imagined Nathaniel riding in the back seat of one of those congregants' cars or sitting with the others in the bed of a pickup. The marks of time his body bore would contradict everything John said. Those marks would promise as the other side of the mountain promises—a shape of indefinite outline, of empty tanks, broken gold lines, and last gasps.

The next morning I woke before the sun rose and making my way down the path to the river in the dim light, I saw the half moon on the horizon, balanced there as though it were the spade of some great shovel ready to pierce the earth for secrets too intimate for the dawn, and there was a story I remembered hearing once, long, long ago, about a time when darkness covered the whole earth. At this time, humans had not yet made much use of their eyes. They listened mostly and did not stray far from their crude dwelling places. These people struggled for sustenance, crawling in the dirt, groping about blindly for whatever they could find, eating insects that burrowed in the soil. Their only tools were sharp, elongated stones they would use to forage for ants, centipedes, grubs, and beetles. Sometimes, they would chance on stores of a rancid sort of honey and distill it into alcohol, mixing it with various roots. The stuff tasted horrid but they binged on it, for the sleep it induced was the only respite to their miserable lives.

Among these people were a man and a woman who gave birth to an extraordinary girl child. She abstained from the creeping and crawling insects and putrid honey booze her parents scavenged, refusing everything with absolute resolve, yet she continued to grow strong. One night, when the entire group, including her parents, were deep in the throes of a drinking binge, the girl slipped away into the night.

When her parents learned she was gone, they lamented aloud to the group. She was trouble from the start, some said. She'll get what's coming to her, another hissed. Always something awry with that one, another stated. The truth was, though, that they all secretly envied her courage and hoped she would die alone in the vast and eternal night that surrounded them.

Then a great thunderstorm swept over the land. Lightning flashed and broke the world apart into a multitude of flickering shapes. There was a lone tree, long dead, or maybe dead from the moment it had first broken through the surface of the earth, and its branches were jagged and gaunt in the cold and sudden light that had split the sky in two.

All the people, including the grieving mother and father, gathered around the tree, for the lightning had struck it and it was burning. None of them had ever seen anything so bright. None had ever seen the singular dance of the flames consuming dead wood, and they all stood in awe.

As the fire began to die down, one of the larger branches fell to the ground with a great crash, a thousand sparks shooting off into the night at the point of impact.

It was the mother first who approached the burning heap. Then the father followed. In the firelight, the whole crowd saw him reach in his pocket and procure the sharp stone. They witnessed him place the point of the stone at the corner of the woman's eye, saw him apply pressure, then dig into it, sawing away at the connective flesh and the veins, dislodging it whole, slick and delicate. Next they saw the father hand the sharpened stone over to the mother, and saw, too, the woman pierce her husband's eye, wrench the stone into the socket, then scoop the eye out in one piece.

Each parent held the other's eye and approached the burning tree. The father held the eye in the fire that still danced at the trunk of the dead tree, then turned to the darkness into which their daughter had wandered. The father hurled his burning eye into that darkness, and it hung there. The whole face of the earth lit up, and all the creeping things hated the light and slithered and crept and scurried away, each in accordance with its anatomy. The light did not last, however, and they crept from their hiding places as darkness was restored. The mother, then, hurled her eye toward the east, where it caught fire and remained suspended there, opposite the eye of the father, which was just now sinking into the horizon. Together, they walked blindly into the wilderness to search for their girl.

John stepped out of the back door of the Matinee and again into the parking lot. It was nearly dark now, but I could see in his hand the large brown paper sack he was carrying back to the car. Mainder still stood in the threshold, watching John and eyeing me in the car.

Mainder was a large man, about the size of John, larger around the belt, broader shoulders, long hair like John's. He wore age as Nathaniel wore it—around the eyes, in the posture, the distinctive weariness that lingers and weighs down every movement, no matter how slight.

John opened the car door and tossed the bag into the back seat. It bounced and the glass bottles inside knocked against one another. With his knee on the seat, he reached into the bag and pulled out a bottle of booze. The scent of whiskey filled the car. Gerome had also given John a few cans of beer. They were still cold, and we sipped them between draughts of the whiskey.

After a while, I heard the sound of cars pulling into the parking lot. It was the congregants. They loitered around their vehicles, hands in jacket pockets, holding up cigarettes. We remained in the car, and after a while, the drink loosened his tongue. He said that those words of theirs—if that's what they can be called—are getting close, with a serpentine crawl, taking miles as dust, since that is the only plausible way of going about it, Jenny, when the needful thing is to look into the split slit eyes of the road and burn up in flames their own miserable hearts, swallow whatever seed they think they've discovered there in the grip of adulthood, a seed like a poisoned coin that can buy neither mercy nor wrath, and therefore must remain fresh in the mouths because we have not yet tasted the cruel grip of time upon the perfect and impossible contours of our alabaster bodies.

Back behind the Matinee there was a lone persimmon tree marking a trail that wound down the hill to a little hollow where two ridges merged. We would drink the booze from Mainder in this little shadowy crevasse, where night seemed to fall earlier and more definitively than upon the open hills above it.

After John had made the exchange at the back entrance, we carried the booze along this trail, down the slope into the hollow. I cleared away some of the dead leaves and we sat down in the mulch. Already, the thick and intricate tangle of the upper reaches of the trees seemed to belong to the night and its substantial element. But there were places where the fleeting light of day still pierced through.

As we sat, I listened to the leaves rustling in the breeze, and somewhere further off, there was the sound of a stream coursing over stone and root on its way, I knew, to join the other streams that all fed into the river. John was reclining against the broad trunk of the tree, one arm crooked behind his head for support.

He extended the bottle to me, its copper contents splashing against the clear glass as I took it in my hand, then to my lips. I felt the whiskey there first in my mouth, then felt its burn down through my throat, then down and further down as it washed over whatever separates night from day in us, or car from road, but it did not settle there in the guts, and continued on, down through my body until it was seeping through my nightgown between my legs, spreading over the thin fabric and weighing it down, then slipping further down into the mulch itself, sliding between the leaves with hardly a sound, then circling the two of us with one eye on the road, as it inclined me now to my hands and knees. John writhed, and I clutched the soft wet ground for traction, and the copper filled my mouth again on the next drink, with no burn now as it slithered away into the woods.

When I woke the next morning I shifted out of John's embrace, lifting myself up off the ground and headed to the bank of the river where I washed the taste of the copper from my mouth, swirling it around over my teeth and tongue, then spitting it back into the current below.

John once told me that he had stumbled upon the famous coppermouth snake one night while reclining in a grassy meadow, gazing up into the stars. He'd heard a rustling in the grass, and when he turned around he saw the thing there staring back at him ready to strike. John leapt up and pounced on the beast. A struggle ensued, and the advantage shifted, now in favor of the snake, now in favor of the man, as they tumbled and rolled around in the grass.

After some time, hours maybe, maybe years, or millennia, John said, it was clear that the two were evenly matched. They disengaged, and both fell back panting, each staring at the other as he tried to catch his breath. The coppermouth snake was the first to speak. He said that because you have neither fled from me nor killed me, and because you have struggled with me without surrendering, I will grant you an answer to the question that most heavily weighs upon your human heart. And in turn, because I neither fled from you, nor killed you, and because I chose to struggle with you without surrender, you shall grant me an answer to the question which most burdens my own animal heart.

John looked the creature over, considered his options, and accepted the serpent's offer, on condition that he himself could ask the first question, a condition upon which the serpent gladly agreed. Now, this confrontation occurred on a spectacular spring night when the moon, in its early phase, appeared in the sky as an elegant crescent accompanied by the whole host of glittering stars, one of those nights when the great dome of the celestial sphere seems to press down upon the dark substance of the night itself and insinuate into the hearts of man the infinite mystery of conscious existence and the feeling that the eyes themselves, in traversing such vast expanses, have at once glimpsed the secret of our most intimate longings for companionship, purpose, and a sense of home, and in the very same miraculous act of vision, shaken to their foundations all our firmest certainties about those very same longings, striking a perfect balance on the scales of the heart of the only creature on earth to have ever gotten into his head the idea to gaze upward out into the cosmos, a balance between gratitude and awe for the miracle of life on one side, and, on the other, sorrow and trepidation for the loneliness that this rare miracle implies.

And so, naturally, John cleared his throat and asked the coppermouth serpent why and how the world came into being.

The coppermouth snake answered that the source of all things is known as the apeiron, or the unbounded, or the boundless. The apeiron is not identical in meaning with the sempiternal, the everlasting, or any atemporal or nonspatial infinitude, but it is related to infinity in some important ways. Its most readily accessible image is that of a circle spiraling, winding, snaking into and through itself.

In the primal state, the boundless is completely undifferentiated, both internally in relation to itself, and externally in relation to anything else. To be internally boundless means two things here, the serpent said. First, it implies that the boundless carries within it all the characteristics of future oppositions, so that there is no boundary, no distinction, for instance, between up and down, before or after, as in a circle, where up eventually goes down and down can only go back up, and where after has already been encountered before, and before will again be encountered after.

Additionally, to be internally boundless indicates that no line can be drawn between part and part and part within whole. Whatever lies within it is equally nothing more than that which it itself is in and is therefore no definite thing but all things mixed together in this wreathe of trembling precosmic volution.

The apeiron was also externally boundless in relation to anything else, which means two things. The first is that all substantial opposites were swallowed up together in the dark corridors of the spiraling apeiron, so that the hot, whose elemental body is fire, lived and died in flashes of perfect flux, only to vanish into the thinnest parts of the thinnest element, air, while the wet, whose element is water, died and lived, coiled and uncoiled, around the dry, whose element is earth. And so the boundless was a spinning circle, complete unto itself, and perfectly whorled around all of being. The helix maintained an equilibrium, consuming and producing itself in cyclical torrents of elemental slaughter, devouring, drowning, freezing, and melting, all mixed up in a pandemonium of ingestion, digestion, mastication, and defecation. The short and long of it, said the snake, is that the boundless was all at once word and deed, head and tail.

At this point in the account, the coppermouth snake paused, and gave a meditative and melancholic sigh. Alas, he said, something so perfect cannot remain so, because time makes eventualities out of that which is not, even if it eventually banishes those eventualities to a past which is not now nor ever again will be. And so eventually, a small part of the apeiron broke away. A split occurred in its immaculate unity, dividing the monistic twine of that boundless circle at the very tip, not unraveling it entirely, but causing a tear sufficient to compromise its coherence. Think of this initial embryonic separation as a fork in the eternal cosmic road upon which the apeiron traveled, the creature said to John. Or as a fork in the tongue, he added.

This renegade piece of the apeiron was filled with a cold, moist, pearlescent mass, suspended in the black mists and noxious vapors that had insinuated themselves between the main part of the apeiron and this divergent concretion. As the apeiron continued to spin, the hot caused these vapors and mists to move more rapidly. They started to smolder.

Soon, the single forked tongue of a flame emerged. It warded off the vapors and mists from the cold, moist mass. The fire grew into a sphere, and wrapped itself around the mass, the way flames will roll with a swirling motion over a piece of timber in those fires you make outside yourselves at night. The fiery sphere coiled around the egg, warming and preserving it, but also fecundating it with the sparks that would eventually become the celestial bodies, whose wheeling courses advance as remnant traces of the original spinning apeiron.

The moon came forth, but caught no flame, and therefore reflected the light of the outer sphere, and served as the eye of the coiled mass, and its phases correspond to the opening and closing of this eye as the source of light gets closer or more distant, becoming crescent to shut out the light when it is close, and becoming a full orb to allow as much light as possible when the source of light is most remote. As the cold, moist mass grew, the heavier parts of it separated from the lighter parts, and thus sea and rocky parts of earth were divided. The protective sphere of fire withdrew as layers of sediment developed over the primal concretion under which the fiery sphere was buried, and these layers of sediment separated sea from land, river valley from mountain, and the whole face of the earth began to take the shape in which you now know it.

When the coppermouth had given his account, both man and snake fell silent. The serpent divined the air with his tongue and stared at the ground as though to let it all sink in. John took a sip of beer and gazed out at the horizon.

The light was changing now as dawn approached. The tall stalks of heather and thin elegant blades of grass that surrounded the conversants began to take on more definitive form in the light, and drops of dew could be seen now nestled deep within the lower tangle of the grasses. There were in the distance the first stirrings of birdsong, and a breeze began to gently caress the tops of the trees that lined the field. After some time, the coppermouth snake slithered forward, fixed his icy reptile gaze upon the man before him and asked his question: Did you really ever think, though you drive and drive, that you'll ever get out of this world alive?

John wandered off to piss. I sat on the ground reeling from the liquor we had carried up the hill behind the Matinee. Its flat roof was partly visible through the branches of the trees. Later on in the evening, some of the old men inside the tavern would appear at Lory's place. They would sit in his garage and drink beer, not speaking, their wretched faces alternatively regarding the radio, the music it spilled through the night, and the aluminum cans of beer they clutched.

The cars down below in the parking lot—we never passed them or saw them on the road at night, never heard them start up and idle even. These cars had been relinquished to the endlessness of this place. The old men inside had perhaps forgotten about that odious breathing mountain. Maybe they had never looked at it, never been looked at by it.

John reappeared into the clearing. He was zipping up his pants, looking into the distance as I had been, at the horizon and the ceiling of cloud hanging over it. The light broke through it. John sat back down on the grass next to me and lit a cigarette. Every moment is a moment too soon, he would sometimes say, and the hour that ends is every hour. He had always stuck with this assertion. Then, after a while, he said, time to move, and we got up from the ground and went back to the car.

Strophic Choral Interlude: The Narrative Tradition in the Music of John Stone

The danger, and I mean to indicate that which informs the richly varied paths toward both bodily and spiritual demise, in approaching the music of John Stone is in the ad hominem condemnation the singer himself seems to invite. The invitation is attributable to Stone's striking appearance, his disagreeable odor, his wild eyes, and the confrontational assertions he is apt to make when in the company of women especially. All of which is most certainly opprobrious in itself.

Yet we are here concerned with his music. This essay attempts to elucidate Stone's relationship to the narrative tradition he has inherited from both the country song and, much more broadly, English narrative poetry, specifically with his masterly manipulation of and his location in the narrative tradition of the country song.

For Stone, the country song is a form whose compositional conventions provide an empty template. Strict adherence to the conventions, on the part of its practitioners, sets up and solidifies certain generic expectations in the listener. For Stone, these expectations have become a source of aesthetic momentum. His songs acknowledge them, only to play against them for sensuously pleasurable purposes. It is in this way that his variations, silences, and obfuscations become meaningful.

Consequently, the music to which his lyrics are set does not stray at all from the conventional demands of the country song. Take for instance "Pray for Us, Mary," gliding along the straight-and-narrow of a honky-tonk shuffle, organized around the verse-chorus duality so pervasive to popular forms. Despite the title's borrowing a phrase from Catholic practices, and the irrefutable absence of Catholicism in these parts, "Pray for Us, Mary" convinces its listener of a teenage experience familiar to anyone having attended the Pentecostal religious services common to southeastern Tennessee and comments indirectly upon such canonized experiences as speaking in tongues, making cheerful noises unto the Lord, and other auditory manifestations of possession by the Holy Spirit.

The song opens with a minor sixth, and begins with a young man at a church service, sitting in what to us seems the familiar prayer circle. Each member of this circle is holding hands. All eyes are closed. We then learn, in the second verse, that the singer, serendipitously finding himself situated next to a young woman in whom he possesses a certain interest, would

> wait for the luring feel
> of your soft teenage hands and pray
> for that gospel power to save.

At this point, in the recording I have heard, the drums and bass guitar enter the song, along a standard four-four shuffle:

> Each Sunday morning came and went,
> and after church, hiding in the van,
> I'd beg for your panty-purring cat.

Then, danger:

> But when the car door came open
> and we blushed for trouble at your mom,
> I was almost in you and wanted to explain

We see the two young Christian lovers in the back seat of the van as they enjoy the fruits of youthful passion, tearing perhaps at one another's clothes, lips wet, hearts beating for the moment of realization. Sadly, however, the door opens and they are exposed. The explanation which follows, though coarse, offers a certain insight into the logic of the young man in the throes of adolescent love. The chorus, driven by a standard twelve-bar blues bass line, reads:

> that when I met Jesus,
> there was only one thing on my mind:
> how to get myself into the virgin
> sitting right in front of my eyes.

Observe the seamlessness of the transition from verse to chorus: that we are shuttled across this compositional mode within a single sentence should draw our attention. Although it may not assist the singer in convincing his audience of the saliency of his argument, it leaves no question about where in the song we are. It is safe to say that the argument ("that when I met Jesus...") most likely fails to elicit the sympathy of the parents who rightfully want to protect the innocence of the church-going daughter. Yet youth prevails, and we learn in the second verse that one night, "with the parents gone," the two are left alone. With the employment of "about ten white lies" on the part of the teen, he gets the girl "into [his] bed." The clothing subsequently comes off, and we become privy to a degree of success achieved in the games of young and innocent love:

> My bedroom hadn't ever known
> anything so smooth against the tongue
> as you let me lick my way home.

The argument is once again revisited, but this time around, because the young man has attained his desired objective, the chorus no longer functions as an argument; it functions, rather, as a justification. Since he met Jesus, there had only been one thing on his mind. The surface remains the same, while the underlying purpose subtly shifts. The listener might be tempted here to ask why this young man has become so single-minded. The explanation presented in the chorus certainly invites such a question. The way I see it, there are two possible answers, neither of which is alone sufficient to satisfy. First, we may attribute this single-mindedness to the quite typical condition of the teenage heart, remembering the fervor with which our young people's desires burn. The second explanation might seem more foreign to Stone's good Presbyterian and Methodist audience. Conventional belief has it that only a "wicked and adulterous generation" seeks signs and wonders for the evidence of things unseen. There is something asinine about demanding from our Lord evidence of his sovereignty through miracles. Faith is a peculiar human faculty in that it thrives off of not-knowing, and faith, we know, suffers from verifications derived from the world of appearance. Yet appearances remain: the Catholic hears so many voluble explications of Mary's virginity that virginity itself assumes a force of its own, and anyone (like the young girl in the song) possessing this quality becomes desirable a fortiori. The Catholic devotee prays to a virgin, contemplates a virgin, gazes upon the image of a virgin, utters the name of a virgin in repetitious invocations. Now the Presbyterians within Stone's range might find this odd. As Southerners, our knowledge of Catholicism is based on what Notre Dame's football team does to the SEC in the autumn months, and my own knowledge, admittedly, does not go much further than this. However, I can safely say that the above mentioned eroticism does not comprise any overt intentions of the Catholic adherent, nor does this sexual dynamic pertain to the psychoanalyst's tenets of displacement, or really have anything to do with the unconscious. No, what we are dealing with here in Stone's song is a flesh and blood version of the spiritual assertion "right before [one's] eyes."

The content of this narrative, as well as its streamlined approach to the climax, partakes of a long tradition of narrative elements in English prosody. What most readily comes to mind is the fabliau antagonism which Chaucer's *Canterbury Tales* presents its readers. In "The Shipman's Tale," for instance, we have perhaps the most pristine example of the popular motif: a woman, finding herself in a debt to unspecified lenders for unspecified reasons, entreats a good-looking young man for money by which to pay her debt. The young man, recognizing opportunity when it presents itself, borrows money from the woman's husband, then gives her that money for the rewards of the body, taking in Chaucer's salacious version "hire in his armes bolt upright," in other words laying her on her back all night long. When the husband comes to collect the money from the young man, the young man informs him that the money has been given to his wife. Then, when the husband confronts the wife about the money in question, she explains to him that she has spent it and that the repayment will be realized in the marriage bed, whensoever he might find himself urged toward its delights.

One fundamental assumption I am making here, one which the reader will not, I hope, find too problematic, is that spiritual currency can be translated rather effortlessly into physical currency. Given this assumption, it is a short step to place Our Lady in the position of the husband: as the benefactor of our spiritual happiness, she holds in her possession the trove which we seekers of pleasure and contentment must plunder, or from which we must borrow. In Stone's song, the young man's amorous pursuits are contingent upon the habitation of Mary, effectively making him a borrower of her wealth. He in turn delivers his borrowed spiritual wealth in bodily form to the young virgin "right before his eyes," who is in turn "licked" but not defeated. She returns to the church, and with certain genuflections, restores the Virgin to her rightful place as everlasting fountainhead of mercy, forgiveness and so forth. Thus spiritual wealth, like its corporeal counterpart, i.e., money, generates itself from the pleasurable cycle described in the song.

It is quite beyond the scope of this Presbyterian's intention to ask if such activities as are here described obtained in the Catholic arena. But I will venture to ask the following question: What would it mean to inquire about the motives behind such foolishness? The assumption is, I believe, for Chaucer's audience as well as for Stone's, that the motivations are self-evident, that they exist right there before our eyes, in the language itself, or in the song itself. To demand an explication of the motivations is to miss the point.

Thus we have the mechanics of (note: not the motivations behind) the narrative action. In "Pray for Us, Mary," the trajectory of the narrative begins with the extramundane and descends upon the mundis of our young hero and heroine with an appeal to reason—grounded in sensuous experience. In counterpoint to the orientation of "Pray for Us, Mary," Stone presents us with another more jangly song entitled "Jean-Luc Bonhomme," in which a revenant exacts revenge upon her husband and executioner, one and the same man. In the voice of a woman (a successful feat of the falsetto), Stone qua revenant finds himself waking up dead:

> When I woke up the next morning
> under the water,
> too scared to open my eyes but too cold to stay under,
> you were the first thing on my mind,
> and when I finally found the shore
> I walked those ten long miles
> back to our home.

The cheerful, easy melody attempts to hide the grim revenge the ghostly bride desires. In the second verse, as additional voices join the action in the background, adding a vocal layer appropriate to the long journey home and the assumed ruminations that would take place on such a journey, the deceased bride arrives. We see what she sees:

> The house was hidden in the dark;
> [there was] just the flicker of the TV set,
> and through the window I stared
> at your guilty silhouette and said

At which point we are escorted into the eerie yet sageful pronouncement of the chorus, whereby the bride's voice confronts her murderous husband:

> Jean-Luc Bonhomme,
> ain't the body a strange thing,
> how it keeps on going,
> how it stays around when we are gone.

At this point, significantly, the guitar parts begin to break down, disintegrating as the bass and drums drop out. The effect is that we become alerted to the contingency of the music upon the story itself: so long as the narrative action moves forward, so, too, can the instruments follow; stop the story, and the instruments lose their *raison d'etre*. Fortunately, the second verse, beautifully wrought, revives the song:

> Well, fish have sucked the wound you left
> and found shelter in my thighs.
> The cold black water bloomed the dress
> I wore my final night.

This description of her appearance should give pause. It is not merely to inform Jean-Luc of the consequences of his crime, but is meant to contrast with the preceding visual image of "the house" in which the revenant finds her husband, "hidden in the dark," the flickering television presaging ghostly revenge. And our singer is generous enough to describe in relative detail how it shall be done:

> So when you're sound asleep,
> alone in our soft bed,
> I'll approach your living lips,
> just to steal your breath.

Now this "just" is of utmost importance to my overall thesis: for if there is no "just," that is, if her motivations were spelled out by some metaphysical need whereby a vengeful apparition thirsted for the breath of the living, then the song would be intolerably prosaic and not at all worthy of our attention. Stone, however, has made the revenant's thievery an accidental by-product of her act of revenge. It is, in other words, the act itself that matters. It is in this way that we are able to leave unanswered the question that the revenant's revenge provokes into being: is the breath of life identical to the voice?

It is here that Stone makes a crucial departure from the narrative tradition. The generic expectations would elicit in the listener the desire to know just why the revenant bride was in the first place killed. After all, what is a story without these fundamental principles of cause and effect? Had she, like Desdemona, "turned to folly" or become a whore? Yet the image urges the question upon us: both Othello and Jean-Luc have killed without shedding blood, "nor scar that whiter skin of hers than snow / and smooth as monumental alabaster." The wound, of course, is singular, one wound, and refers to the virginal flower (evident in the proximity to the thighs and in the figuration of flowers evoked in the blooming dress) that has been left only insofar as it has been abandoned and never touched. This submerged corpse certainly strikes us as picturesque in death: the dress in the water, shelter for the fish.

The revenant's comment that she will do it "just to steal your breath," supplies us with our own air to breathe. These are the words spoken as effects of moments of rapture, just as in "Pray for Us, Mary," we can responsibly imagine certain teenage effusions in that bedroom, when the bra and panties come off, and the sky is unfurled, the great persimmon of life itself blossoms or blooms as the wedding dress at the moment of submersion.

All of these forces come to a fantastic illuminatory head in what I believe to be Stone's chief accomplishment, a song entitled "If You Like It Black." The victim's name is Fernaline

(Fern in the first verse, where the terms of intimacy must be established). The song opens at a motel off the interstate:

> I stuck Fern with the bill at the cheap motel
> that had risen up from the ashes of
> I-35 at 2:09
> in the middle of a hot and fatal Sunday night.
>
> I cuffed her to the bed, sprayed lighter fluid
> all over the brown formica counter tops.
> Then I danced a dance for Fernaline
> that should have lifted my self-esteem.
>
> The bureau mirror held the burning lights
> of Oklahoma City and an exit sign
> so with the freedom of being done with love
> I ex-ed that girl with a match and a few dirty words.

We do not know why the city, from which the couple has presumably fled, is burning. It is certainly figurative, as there is nothing to be gained from the suggestion that Fernaline and the first-person narrator are escaping an actual city on fire. The circumstances behind their venturing onto the freeway are left open, and one may or may not be inclined to fill in that which Stone leaves open. We are immediately thrust into the chorus (and thrust rather uncomfortably ahead into the narrative action by a transition to a minor third):

> Since I've been driving all alone,
> I've heard it said much too often:
> "If you like black pussy,
> then [head on out to] New York City."

The chorus invites speculation as to its meaning, and only when the listener makes it through the following guitar solo, remarking upon the chorus itself as a way, perhaps, of allowing for a moment of contemplation, only until the prowess of the instrumental solo has been withstood can our uncertainty regarding the action described in the chorus be addressed, and this is precisely what happens in the succeeding verses:

> Now I see her face in each car window
> in the Ozark fir and painted smiles
> of billboard signs above the phone lines
> that blackly cut up the Midwest's open sky.
>
> Now my sweating palms [are] on the steering wheel,
> now I break for a ghost and I lose control,
> now the caving in of aluminum—
> the surrender to debris waiting our every end.

We imagine skidding tires screech as the swerving automobile finds its bodily conclusion against another unfortunate car, or the freeway median, the singer's capitulation to his fate as it is played out in an instant, just as Fernaline's ghost only haunts him in the other cars' windows and the billboards and so forth, and we hear once again the chorus, which makes more sense now that we can imagine the thin trickle of the radio (for those who want a literal picture) or merely the lonely freeway's propensity for conjuring voices, especially those that have been wronged:

> Since I've been driving all alone,
> I've heard it said much too often:
> "If you like black pussy,
> then [head on out to] New York City."

Black, of course, refers to Fernaline's charred body, the memory of which haunts the singer, who is fleeing from the motel scene of his crime. The suggestion to head east is a reversal of sorts; it is the hell of the American solution to head to the edenic west. We only have to throw a cursory look at Waylon Jennings's "California Sunshine," or at Steinbeck's *Grapes of Wrath,* to realize that westward lies possibility, riches and freedom, for the continent is endless in that direction. To go east, however, is to regress.

What is missing in these songs is precisely that which makes them interesting. These songs say nothing about the motivations effecting the narrative action. The argument about seeing a virgin "right before my eyes," is not an argument at all, nor is it meant to be. That the young man, dancing his dance before the handcuffed Fernaline on the bed, has failed to lift his self-esteem, is no reason to strike the match and utter a few dirty words. The country song, then, is conceived by Stone as a set of actions disconnected from their motivating factors. It takes a sensitive soul to derive pleasure from these kinds of stories, and the imagination never demands an answer why from its own productions.

Four

JE NE SAIS QUOI

It was dark when we got back to the car. I looked at the wooded hill where we had been drinking. It was a solid mass of shadow now, and it seemed impossible for us to have been there just moments ago, swallowed by those shadows but somehow having found a way to escape them.

We stood in the parking lot among his ragged congregation. Some were standing around their own vehicles. A couple of the larger, meaner-looking boys were sitting on the hood of John's Firebird. They scowled at us as we passed into the light cast by the sign of the Matinee. John lowered his head and walked before one of them with no acknowledgment of his presence.

He was standing at the door of his car when one placed his hands on John's shoulder, spun him around and stared into his face. The other kid came around from behind John and shoved him in the shoulder. John tensed up but immediately stepped back and shrugged off the offense, everything in him becoming slack, the way a paramedic, leaning over a body whose life had just moments ago hung in the balance, might sigh and slacken when the thing is decided. John reached into the car for one of the bottles Gerome Mainder had sold him earlier. He pulled up the cork, took a sip and offered it to them. The larger one, who had remained silent, swatted it away. It fell to the ground, and there was that unmistakable sound of the whiskey gurgling from the mouth of the bottle. John looked down at it but did not move. He caressed the larger one's head, his thumb lingering on the cheekbone. The kid glared at him and brought his hand up to swipe it away, but John had already removed it by the time contact was made.

He took a step back, out of arm's reach, and addressed his audience. Consider that it takes the earth an entire day to rid itself of the sun, he said. The sun is therefore its gravest thought. The sun is its only thought. The earth waits. It might or might not turn as it waits. It eats the bodies of humans and animals, of plants and fish. It eats stone, glass, and mountain. It drinks blood and water. He pointed to the ground where the bottle lay, and said the earth even partakes of spirits every once in a great while. When finally free of that single duplicitous shining thought, and the sheath of night slips over her surface, the earth shivers in her panties and slips into celestial bed with the moon. When she eats up the soft caresses of all the nocturnal animals moving on the surface of her body, we must ask ourselves, has she gotten what she wanted? Is she satisfied with the taste of dirt on the gut, or does she long for more? Why else would the sun rise then, just a few hours after that girl has been tasting and enjoying the carnal fruits of night?

If we were to slip out into the void, the sun would shine right through us. If we were to exult in the distance of the mountain, our eyes would burn out of their sockets, fall to the ground with that enameled wish that makes mankind find again the same steps he'd taken the day before, find safety in the resilience of four firm walls, arranged according to the dictates not of the heart but of the stone, not of the Firebird but of the gleam in a cop's eye. We do not understand distance until we repeat its course and draw it near. A mile does not lose its capacity as a standard of measure just because the highway doesn't end. Money does not lose its power just because it ceases to become scarce. Miles, money, years, words—these abstractions will not mingle with your beautiful bodies. Miles are simply what is given to the car to eat. Money is simply what is given to the guts to drink. Years are what is given when we meet each other in bed at night, near the fire or out in the weeds by the river. And words—I'm beginning to think, Jenny, that you've yet to understand a goddamn thing I've said.

The next morning when I walked back up the path from the river, I saw the congregants there in the camp. There were a few boys gathered around the pit of ash, slouching as they watched another on his knees digging up the fire. There were two girls sharing a cigarette, seated in the grass, looking out vacantly. There was a couple, intertwined still on the ragged blanket they shared, the girl wearing cut-off jeans that showed her smooth tan thighs, her legs wrapped around her partner's waist, her arms around his bare torso, her chin leaning on his shoulder. The breeze stirred her long silky hair. She seemed to sink further into the gulf that separated her from the boy she held in her arms. Despite the rigid, chiseled stillness in the stone of their being, they became like creeping shadows from whom all solidity and assurance had departed, and the certainty of the body faded at the edges of the figure they formed there together.

And lying about camp were others, tangled together, moving always as flames move, never at rest, retreating from the certainties of vision, there being no fluidity to their movements, even as one now brought a can a beer to his mouth to drink, or another inhaled the smoke of a cigarette, or yet another ran a hand through his long hair and cracked a smile of no consequence. It was as though, having been caught in these various stages of adolescent change, their physical being had been denied those bodily continuities that enable us to perceive the subtler truths of motion.

Yet even their stillness was transient, a lie, John says, like that of the maggot whose writhing presence startles us when we catch a glimpse of it and think it has appeared suddenly, that it has crept up on us while we were busy negotiating a turn or savoring the feel of the tires gripping the road, or skidding a bit in the birthing fluids that are spread over its asphalt surface, like the small black cat I remembered having heard a story about, who had fled the hardships of life in the valley, and hoped to make a new life atop a mountain he had only glimpsed in dreams.

This cat climbed for days over the saddlebacks of the lower hills, crouching to hide when he saw the hoary old mountain goat and the skittish mule deer. When night fell at the end of the first day of his journey, he heard the howls of wolves echoing through the ravines and slowed his pace, since everything that is far becomes near at night, even the hot breath of a wolf. He followed the arc of the moon and found it swallowed up by a great cathedral of stones whose spires seemed to hold up the black sky. As dawn approached, he saw that he had reached the top.

He leapt nimbly from the smaller stones up to the larger ones, gazing into the unlit depths of the crevasses that separated them. When he could go no higher he turned and surveyed the great distances his new position commanded. He saw before him the sweeping valley, the streams that cut through it, and the foothills rising up from it, as though they were merely the creases and folds of a soft blanket, or ripples in a body of water that had been suspended in time. He watched the shadows of the larger hills above move over the land, coupled in some virginal corner of the imagination with the sweep of the sun overhead, as it reached its own pinnacle, imperceptible because it refused any rest there before its descent toward the horizon.

Evening approached, and the small black cat, shaking himself free of the grip of this magnificent vision, considered his situation. He was hungry, tired, and quite alone.

In the days that followed, he explored the area, napped fitfully and tried to ignore his hunger, for he was having little luck in securing food. One night, in the deep hours just before dawn, he was awakened by a terrible felid growl that echoed throughout the boulders of that mountaintop sanctuary. It was like nothing he had ever heard before. He crouched further into his hiding place among the rocks and waited. As the night thinned out into the gray light of dawn, he saw a great shadowy figure, appear then vanish, as it leapt from one rock to another in effortless strides.

This shadow belonged to the ferocious mountain lion. Fresh blood stained the whiskers of the cougar, and bits of fur and flesh from a fresh kill were still lodged in his claws. The cougar turned and locked eyes with the small black cat hiding in the shadows. The two creatures regarded one another there, and in that moment, the whole fearsome world became concentrated in the icy stare that joined them. The small cat tried with all his might to remain still, trusting in the confluence of the shadows around him and the dark hues of his own coat, but his strength in invisibility faltered, and he began to tremble, slightly at first, then uncontrollably until he could no longer hold the other's gaze.

The small cat started to back away, but his stomach turned and his throat tightened. He became dizzy and dug his claws into the ground for traction against the wave of nausea that was sweeping over him now. His eyes, still locked with those of the cougar, began to fill with tears. His mouth became dry, and his stomach turned again. He could feel something pulsing there inside him, pounding in a strange rhythm against his insides, expanding through his entire being, then, a moment later, called back to its source. The cat began to cough and wretch—there was something inside him, the nausea having separated from his own inner corridors now and struggled to get out, up through the throat, on the tongue, and the small black cat felt his mouth being compelled open by what filled it, and he spilled it all there on the ground before him—it was a creature he had never seen before, without fur, covered in bloody pink skin that shone in the light of dawn, and it was writhing its head rolling on a neck too feeble to hold its weight. Then this strange, misshapen creature opened its mouth and spilled forth a terrible, prolonged shriek that shook the foundations of the earth, causing all the other animals, both great and small, to stop in their tracks. Remembering his fear, the small black cat looked up from the wailing mess before him. The cougar was gone.

Charles Shedd, Universal Drinking Buddy, Is Dead at 59

Charles Shedd, a regular at the local tavern who enjoyed billiards, darts, and Jimmie Rodgers, died sometime early Monday morning in Graysville.

The cause of death was cardiac arrhythmia, said the examiner at Rhea County Hospital in Dayton.

Last seen as he left a bar off Highway 27, Mr. Shedd was found dead in the driver seat of his Oldsmobile by the tavern's manager, Gerome Mainder. "Saw him there sitting upright," said Mr. Mainder, "thought he was waiting to sober up or maybe just thinking." Mr. Mainder proceeded to the car to offer his customer a ride. When Mr. Shedd was unresponsive, the bartender called the paramedics. Shedd was pronounced dead upon arrival.

In 1954, Charles Shedd was bequeathed by his father-in-law Florin Carpet and Cleaning Co., which included a thousand-foot-square warehouse adjoined by a small retail store off Highway 27. Later that same year, however, the company was handed over to Mr. Shedd's brother-in-law, Gus Drake, though Shedd stayed on as an employee.

Florin Carpet and Cleaning Co. serviced many homes in the Graysville area and supplied local businesses with a wide variety of flooring. Throughout the mid-sixties the inventory was expanded to include linoleum, vinyl, and ceramic tiles, a wide array of grouts and mortars, as well as basic home repair tools.

Carpeting, by far, was Florin Co.'s specialty. Mr. Shedd was knowledgeable about the latest trends in carpeting, and possessed a great command of both the classic and most up-to-date materials, though it often required a great deal of forthrightness to get the information out of him. "Polyester, acrylic, wool," said James Fern, a co-worker of the late Mr. Shedd. "You name it and he knew it."

One source said, "It is thanks to Shedd that many of the homes in our area have been able to keep up with the latest styles."

Charles Ely Shedd was born on March 12, 1918 in Graysville, Tennessee. He spent his childhood here, with four brothers and three sisters. He graduated from Sam Davis High School in 1937. Five years later, he fought in the 45th Infantry Division in Sicily and later in northern Italy.

After his time in the service, Mr. Shedd returned to Graysville to work for his father-in-law's carpet company. In the beginning of his career, he performed multiple duties, from manning the cash register of Florin's retail store to installing carpets in homes. Eventually he focused his energies on the demands of the warehouse. "Charlie got along alright in strangers' homes," remembered one co-worker, "but didn't really take to interacting with others." Mr. Shedd found the solitude of the warehouse, the forklift, and great broadloom rolls of carpet more to his liking.

In the autumn of 1972, however, an accident occurred. A load of broadlooms toppled over, injuring Mr. Shedd's back and leaving him unable to drive the forklift or manage heavy weights.

In the last years of his life, Shedd reliably took up a seat at the local tavern. His friendship was enjoyed by many of the regulars. "It was like he really opened up here," said one friend, referring to Mr. Shedd's unexpected volubility, after years of relative silence at home and in the Florin warehouse. "Kept to himself mostly in the day," said Mr. Mainder from behind the bar, "but once he got going talking, he could convince you the sky was falling."

Charles Shedd is survived by his wife, Jane, a daughter, and four siblings presently residing in Knoxville.

Evening was falling and we were working on the booze Mainder had sold us. I heard the cars of the congregation pull up on the gravel and watched them pile out. They looked thirsty, leaping out of the bed of a pickup one drove, swinging their doors open at once, the music spilling from the cars, some of them in a sort of easy palpitant embrace, clanging car keys against their worn-out denim, spitting into the gravel of the parking lot, others holding cigarettes and beers.

They milled about at first, then loosely gathered into a far corner of the lot, just within reach of the reddish light of the sign of the bar to settle into their drinking. There they congregated, drank, and cackled. John staggered among them, passing them bottles, taking sips of their drinks, hits of their cigarettes, talking to them as he passed by, leering at some, clenching others on the shoulders, encouraging them all to drink up and enjoy themselves. Share your sorrows, he said, swigging from the bottle then raising it above his head to see the evening sky through the copper remains.

After some time, they grew restless and rough with each other. A scuffle broke out, but then quickly broke into laughter. One of the girls was whimpering and wandered off alone into the dark. As the night progressed, and everyone was reeling from the drink, John established some order among them, got worked up into a frenzy about some phantom voice he thought he had heard creep out. They crowded together, and John paraded around before them, saluting the night, told them the day had shed its skin and they should do the same. He hissed and bellowed, and they tried to do the same. They could mimic his fervor but not his meaning.

Then he stopped pacing and all fell silent for a moment. He had gotten an idea. He was, he said, going to teach them their first real word. He commanded them to follow him through the parking lot. Some followed, some hung behind to watch. The little group followed him to the nearest car and stopped. It was a pickup truck, twenty or so years old, rusted wheel wells, mud caked on it, bits of cut grass clinging to it.

He knelt down near the tailgate and ran his finger over the name emblazoned on it. Chevrolet, he said, slowly, sounding out the words. He looked up at the closest kid—one of the boys with a vicious look, bruises on his neck just above his flannel shirt collar—and motioned for him to come closer. John pointed at his own mouth, then made a sweeping gesture from his chest to throat and mouth, his hands unfolding as they moved upward, a gesture meant to depict the genesis of a meaningful utterance, a process, he said, that could be as pleasant as vomiting into a bush. He pointed at the word and slowly repeated the car's name, Chevrolet.

Looking at the name, the kid took a deep breath, nodded his head and tried to spill this word out, but all that came was that same raspy noise that had always made these kids unintelligible. John was patient, though, and repeated the syllables one at a time. Another one of the congregants crouched down nearby, frail, his eyes bloodshot. He tried, but failed again to make a sound that in any way resembled the one John had uttered.

John walked to another car, picked out another kid from the crowd, brought him near and read the word slowly, Buick, Buick, Buick, emphasizing the motion of the mouth, the tongue, the teeth and lips, caressing the silver aluminum logo on the panel of the car, repeating it again, putting his face closer to it, gazing even into its flat white surface, too dirty to give off a reflection. Again no resemblance, just the muttered mantra that always spilled from their mouths.

John swatted the car and got on his feet. Someone handed him a beer, and he escorted the group to the next car, then the next, and still more. Each time, though, the attempt to speak failed to produce the sound John had wanted to hear, becoming glassy in the mouth of another, words whose concrete body clung to another concrete body and could not be torn from the faulty apparatus of speech.

The group had visited almost every car in the gravel parking lot of the Matinee. By now, most of his congregation had wandered off, unable to reproduce the language which came so fluidly to John, at any time of day, with greater amounts of verbal agility, in fact, and newer, more savage tones all the time. I imagined those words taking bodily form, gliding out the window at night when we will have driven down the highway, chasing the bit of light our own headlights throw out onto the road or chasing nothing at all, alleviating the car of the pervasive stillness of this place, lashing out at that stillness with each mile per hour, disavowing its silence with the rabid protestation of the engine.

John was running his hand across the body of another car now, a black sedan, an Oldsmobile. The sign of the Matinee was reflected there, curving up with the contours of the car, giving it a luxurious and sinister appearance, as though it had driven past important places. I looked around and saw there were only a few of us still following him around the parking lot. John kept the palm of his hand on the body of the car, pressed it against the surface, gently, and remained there for some time, not saying anything. His eyes were closed, and I could see his hand slightly shaking.

Sometimes at night when we are driving down the highway and he falls silent, I touch him, on his arm, or his hand on the steering wheel. He welcomes it, he says, and thanks me, saying sentimental things about his Firebird, how it would refuse to rise from the ashes if he had not coaxed it out with the scent of his alcohol-poisoned blood, the only thing it wants to drink, the only thing that can make it fly down this highway at night, Jenny, you understand, even if I don't, because, he says, it is a lie that we must surrender what we value most, in order to retrieve it again, know it anew, a lie that tells us to rid ourselves of that which cannot be known in order to know it in its truth, and this lie is the sustenance of fools and highway patrolmen and the necromancy of paramedics, for there is nothing that should escape our touch, our gaze, our thirst, our somatic dive into the surface of a world whose surface drinks up its depths at eighty, ninety, a hundred miles an hour, and we should surrender not a single shred of what has passed through our hands, not a single word that has been swayed into being by the pulpy, verbal musculature of the throat and heart, no, we should rather seize it all in our frail talons, every bit of unctuous blacktop, every bit of the banquet laid at miles per hour and thieved at night by the clutch, chassis, axle, and piston, and the escalating peril of throttle, and the booze that agitates it all into a precise, funereal order that shall be achieved never again on this goddamned earth nor in the headlight glow of heaven, Evenene.

John knelt beside the Oldsmobile. We waited to hear the name of the car. His eyes opened and he said he hoped someone could say this beautiful name, said that he longed to hear it graze the lips of someone other than himself, just once. Then he searched the faces of those who remained and without taking his hand off the steel insignia, he lifted his eyes to me. He said, you, Jenny, try to say its name.

He was still looking up at me. I thought what the hell and stepped forward and knelt down on the gravel parking lot beside him. I looked up at the insignia on the trunk of the car. I had seen these same cars here, parked haphazardly, signs of quick and easy abandonment by their drivers with eyes for the door of the bar, each night after each next morning, or in between them, when John and I walked up the hill after making our purchase from Mainder, but I had never really looked at them with any close attention to detail.

The elegant design seemed to resemble a shield, a symbol from a different era, evocative of a different order of things, a primordial time before cars, even though John has always maintained there was no time in world history when there was neither human nor car, though the car took various forms, adopted various erotomotive cloaks. I saw that he was gazing with me into the rich, delicate details of the Oldsmobile script. I caught his reflection in the gloss of the car as he spoke the single word. Then he repeated the name, emphasizing the rush of consonants in the middle of the word, drawing out the vowels, repeating it again, with reverence, allowing the syllables to unfold according to their natural design and hang in the air for a moment while they coalesced into a single name that sweetened as it lingered there between us, a process full of contradiction because the name only becomes whole as an echo of its parts no longer on the lips.

Then it was my turn to repeat it. I breathed in. With my eyes taking in at once John's reflection in the black sheen of the car and the supple script of the name it carried, I leaned forward, took a breath and started to say the name.

But I have never heard a story of a name like Oldsmobile spilling from the mouth of a girl, river, buzzard, radio, star, or mountain. Cars do not give birth to other cars, John said the next night when we were driving down the highway in the mute black void that pressed up against the white lines painted on the asphalt. For the car there is no generation, regeneration, hips, plugs, condoms, screws, cords umbilical, chords triadic, cords copped executive, no seats saturated of placenta, no head staunched of blood, brow of sweat, gutsack of piss, nor that single, sudden attack of the world's helioflammated infecund air against pure lung to pry it into a life of an ever-diminishing number of breaths, eyed by paramedics aglow in the circumfluent beams of red and blue. No, cars are not born at all, never have been, but simply transmutate, appear like gold-leaf feathers tumbling down upon a corpse to cover the violet blush in the veins of chaos and sink down into the watery substrata, too far for the eyes to reach, too fast for the churning mind to stabilize.

At certain speeds, though, the Firebird hammers up a gash that can in and of itself sexually ignite it, all the underpinnings are in place, all candles lit in the regions whose musk you can smell at night, a flickering flame that has doubled in the fingertips of the poor bastards on the assembly line. Cops sometimes dangle it before the nose just to make the eyelids sink, make the heart flutter for the hope of some excitement and discord.

He was trying to ease my mind off of the word I had choked on, the Oldsmobile, which still lay in my guts somewhere but too deep to bring up to the surface. In the passenger seat, I slouched and drank, letting my head swim through what it could, letting my eyes rest on the sight of the void beyond the reach of the headlights. He talked about Old Man Lory, about the victory we all hold close to us, ale and pilsner, suck and awe, Jenny, nuances that flee as soon as you try to grasp them, Evenene, not because they're forbidden or even elusive, but because of some law set down in another world, another time, up some bastard sheriff's ass maybe, written in piss and vinegar, goddamn it, scratched out onto stone with the brill of a porcupine caught in a trap, alive, weary, diligent enough in death to animate his shrill cries with the only authentic motivation this whore mother earth has ever seen, traced back to the original motivation, which can only be automotivation and its soft spark-plug touch, for the combustible engine is a jealous god, to be tuned to the most harrowing and mournful pitch, which no verminuitive dying animal can ever approximate, since the fuse-box cadence is so damned lonesome that we could relight night after night whatever stars might have faded out since their last blazing thrust toward the besoiled ground of this valley.

He talked of the ground, of the soil as a harlot. He named the insects one by one, filing these names into an ugly kingdom with no leader, only the everlasting playground of the corpse that has lost its way. He talked of boundaries, imposed arbitrarily onto the human body once it reaches a certain age, and the brutal cathedral the living soil makes of it once its transmission has dropped.

He spoke of the arcana of the directions, east, west, north, and south, all kept in place by some hand whose palm is too withered to be read, a palm that has never once had to grasp a steering wheel nor be crushed undertire, nor skid through the membrane to escape the cursed bitch its mother's womb.

He swore, then checked the rearview mirror. Even in the pitch darkness, I could still just make out the faint outline of the mountain. He said: that damned hill is a bump in the road and a noose in the trunk. Not a word of wrath of weight in dew. No word is that important, Jenny, and you are lovely. No tyranny from above, no tyranny from below, just demonic thirst and kindling, just dew on the soft fresh ground for your soft bare feet.

We were on the highway now heading for Lory's. There was the sound of the engine as the incorporation of exploding, churning, trembling raucous machinery, which is how the gaskets bind the darkness to the miles and mile to the hour.

I once heard that chaos was born before the void. Others have said they are twins, since nothing happens as it all happens, for instance, the sound of the engine folding over onto itself before it seizes its own self-expansion in order to flaunt the breaches in the spectrum of perceptible phenomena, then receding as it draws toward our shared counterpoint in vision, auditory and tactile sensation, scent and thirst. I imagine it splitting open the dashboard and getting at the secret at the heart of our motion which is nothing and nowhere at once.

John believes that chaos is younger than anything else, even drunkenness and sex. Chaos, he says, was born from the void and has the advantage of youth over the void, which is all at once its mother and father, brother and sister, lover and murderer, piston and crank. At night, when sleeping and waking stumble into each other and give way to the coiled black eye beyond the reach of the headlights, that birth becomes substance and sanguine, the way the branches of the trees, the weeds and grass, the moths and bugs, road signs and trash all take on definitive weight when the headlights cast their glow out onto the things of the world, giving them shadows they had never asked for.

Then he told me a story. Long ago, he says, the void decided to fashion a body for itself. It groped blindly about in a deadly veil of gasoline fumes. Certain liquids—radiator fluid, coolants, beer—mingled in its grip, and when it closed on this mixture, it hardened and became solid. The mixture then lent motion to the engine. Things began spinning into place—axles, tires, steering columns, gears, fan belts. The gases this machine expired in its act of breathing were embraced by hot metal and trapped in a chamber of virginal lure. The fire, transformed, found its way out, and the machine idled.

But this idling did not satisfy its internal logic, so the mechanical substrata turned over, and the car lurched forward and steadied its pace before picking up speed. In order to realize this need to move, it created space through which to move. But mere spatial relations were insufficient to the concept of motion built inside it. Space constituted a totality, but this totality was simultaneous. What was needed was succession, a force that could tear apart the whole and drop these parts into the gaping mouth of the engine. And so it created time also, in order to balance out the purely tactile sensation of getting from one place to another.

The void, according to John, thrived from what we now call miles per hour. The more it ate, the more it wanted. It accelerated and this acceleration gave shape to its contours. But as it raced through its own nothingness it became definite, individuated and positive, all of which contradicted its nature as the void.

Soon, the appetites of this body it had made became too concrete, and the void decided to annihilate itself. Control was lost, the grip of the tires loosened from the road, and the body spun, rolled over and slammed into a ditch. The wreckage was as absolute as the void itself, its parts cast in all directions, some settling into place finally as the heavenly bodies, others cast into the body of the earth, scarring it and giving it its deep valleys and high mountains and all its other luxuriant features, everything acquiring its sexual character from this progenitive stream of wreckage, whose own internal frictions sought to resolve themselves upon whatever body lay closest to them.

John says that this cosmogonic erotomotive climax had enough force to delimit the age and general trajectory of the life of the individual men and women born of it. Our lifespan would be, this automotive logic determined, the length of the scars that remained in the earth when the bits of auto scraps smashed into it. In his mind, then, one and the same boundary determines how far a person can wander from his point of origin in miles and how long that person can continue to steal breath from the world in hours.

The river is one of these wounds in the earth. At its end it swallows itself, doubling back somewhere downstream, where it has erased even the memory of its own origin from the bits of windshield glass and twisted metal from the primary movement of the original cosmic wreak.

The momentum of the river still inscribes this chaos onto the body of the earth, and Nathaniel is there to feed off it. The poison his body spits up through the pores taunts the thunderclouds and the buzzards above, invites talon and torrent. His head goes under the water and his name is erased from the world. His head appears again and his name is restored to him. All other corporeal remains of the creatures grow weary and ripen. He borrows from the river its insensate madness to keep moving.

All the other creatures are too sensible to plod along toward the next altar, the next gas station, the next abomination, the next purchase, having no alms, but only the long drive from work at the end of the day, to the bar, then the even longer drive back home.

John says that the congregants re-enact the original wreck themselves when spread out on their quilts near the fire, gasping, thrusting, bursting as they drive up against and into one another's youthful bodies. It is possible, he tells them for encouragement, to thrust and squirm to bear the brunt of it, to come and sweeten, to yield and sigh, to give names to every part of the body at night and to forget those names in the morning, to throw them back into the face of the void, with the impudence of eternal youth, to hurl them into the river, or into the dancing blaze of the campfire, to even deposit them somehow into one of the many mouths of our lovers, where they can sink to the bottom of human concerns and drown there, as the guts and fluids of the body, now sated, are preparing for the new stillness of another stretch of highway sleep.

When I woke the next morning I went to the riverside, knelt down and washed my mouth out with the crisp cool water there. Whatever sleep does to the mouth it does to the word. Whatever words we have are had at night, John says. A word like Oldsmobile could not last through the night, even if it had lain mangled on the hard surface of the parking lot or unformed in the throat. Even if it had been washed away by the rest of the liquor John had gotten from Mainder and forgotten as we drove the road together to Lory's house to sit and drink in the garage, to shed the heat and listen to the old men talk up against the limits of what they couldn't say, then it would have been something that did not remain.

Lory's garage faces the road and casts its faint light there, just enough to make visible the long-stretching yellow lines and the weeds on the embankment. The trees on the far side of the road are gaunt but not barren. Their leaves mass together and block out the night sky.

John says the tree is a monster with a thousand leaves for eyes that never close. In daylight, these eyes watch only the sun. But at night, having nothing else to look at, they turn the mute terror of their vision onto humanity. Here they stand as witnesses to the old men who sit on lawn chairs, stools, and old coolers and drink their beer and listen to the radio.

Lory is there, situated in the threshold of the garage, his back turned to the darkness outside. Chuck Shedd is always there, too, turning loose tobacco to ash, running his hand through his gray hair, working his jaw in silence. There are others and they could have any name, Vince, Lee, Tim, Bruce, nimbly rolling cigarettes, lighting each his own, gripping each his own can of beer, closing and opening each his eyes according to his own sense of what the music and night together might fend off.

Like the congregation back at camp, these old men do not have the talent of speech. They mutter to themselves, each equipped with his own private way of pairing thoughts and things with the trembling of the vocal gear, for no other reason maybe than to drop the stoney, broken-up contents of the mind into the great gulf that has separated the body from the engine and both from the distances neither can ever again travel, distances where most thoughts get lost in the endless avenues of its physiology, the turns and dead ends of the viscera. The drink doesn't loosen up their tongues, and the music delivers no one up to revelry. There is no bed of memories they can fall toward or rely on. The present moment and all its mortifying stillness is soft though, and it is here that they live.

The garage itself feels immense in its capacity for quietude and languor. It is lit by a bare light bulb overhead, which sometimes flickers with fatigue and makes the presence of the body more secure in its physical being simply because it has appeared and disappeared so many times. The borders of the garage are faint. When I am sitting among them, I sense shelving loaded with tool boxes, old glass jars full of stray nails, screws, bolts, springs and washers, open cans of oil rimmed with the muck of ash, dead insects, sawdust held together by viscous liquids that have now hardened. I sense ashtrays that have had their fill, beer cans that were once full and never again will be, calendars faded and jaundiced, pages torn at the corners, whose pictures depict breath-taking vistas, the engineering feats of mankind, bridges, temples, and pistons. I sense broom handles, rakes and hoes, baseball bats and pick-axes leaning in the corners, connected with cobwebs, the wood of these implements for investigating the earth dried out and splintered. I sense all of this but can't verify it because the reach of the single bulb does not illuminate the walls of the garage.

I do know, however, that somewhere back in the vague recesses of Lory's garage lies the hollow remnant body of a car, propped up by cinder blocks under its axle, no hood to hide the engine block. The car has no doors. There is only a single seat. Bits of foam spill from the tears in the upholstery. The floorboards of the car have been worn away, and on the seat lies the gearshift, a few bolts, a crescent wrench.

There is a dog with no pedigree and no more hunts in his legs who sometimes sleeps under the car, cooling himself on the cement floor of the garage. When one of the old men occasionally gets up from his seat, the dog becomes attentive, his eyes following the movement, and if the man happens to stumble in the car's direction or toss a beer can at it, the dog emits a low growl, only its eyes and upper lip disturbed into motion.

Sometimes John gets up out of his seat next to Lory and walks over to it, inspects its insides, runs his free hand over the fender, the mirrors, the gaskets. Sometimes, too, he picks up a wrench and some pliers, hunches over its insides and works on the thing. He doesn't talk to it the way he talks to his own car but works brusquely and without conviction. I can tell he detests the thing for its ruin, for its having surrendered to age and use.

That night of the next morning I rode in the passenger seat of John's Firebird back to the house. The old-timers were there, drinking in the garage where he worked on his car. The dog was resting its chin on the ground at Chuck's feet. John wielded a wrench, waving it back and forth as he talked over the music playing from the little radio propped up against a cinder block.

The garage door was open, and the night's sound would emerge between songs, filling in what would otherwise be silence. The light from the open garage reached out past the driveway, and just touched the treeline on the far side of the street.

There's something utterly perverse, John was saying, about an animal that responds to the human voice with anything but fear. He pointed the wrench at the dog. Some kind of shame in heeding the human's call. The pitch, the timber, the inflection—and all other vocal flourishes, unique to our own anatomy, tell the animals that a poor creature with attenuated senses and ears stuffed full of cotton is coming, just like our heavy clumsy stumbling step tells all the nocturnal animals that some upright creature full of whiskey and piss is coming around the bend, don't give chase, don't even move because you won't be seen, and now he was waving his wrench, don't even blink or whine or bark or breathe, because we'll blast on by and not see a goddamn thing. Alas, he said, sighing, the deer darts off. And the rabbit flees. And the cat scurries away. And the old hateful coppermouth slithers out of sight and mind. That is why only mice can live among us. Why the lost-soul cicadas are our music. That is why coyotes will sometimes sneak up on a drunk hollering out behind the Matinee. And it is why in old stories I've heard the dog, as the protector of mankind, has tried to correct this mistake by eating the scraps without protest.

Shedd muttered something, his voice complicated by the absence of teeth, and raised his beer can to drink. After a while, he stood, stretched, yawned, and left the garage into the night.

Charles Shedd, Universal Drinking Buddy, Is Dead at 59

Charles Shedd, a regular at the local tavern who enjoyed billiards and Ray Price, was found dead in the weeds off the shoulder of Highway 27 early Monday morning. He was 59 years old. The cause of death was blunt trauma to the head, presumably suffered when he made contact with the pavement. Authorities are looking into the possibility of a hit-and-run scenario.

Last seen leaving a friend's house some time after midnight, Charles Shedd had declined an offer for a ride home and told his drinking buddies that he was sober enough to make the walk alone.

Charles Shedd had a complicated, antagonistic relationship with automobiles in general. In the mid-1960s, Mr. Shedd was involved in a number of traffic accidents, one of which ended in a fatality. Although no criminal charges were pursued, these incidents demanded a severe toll upon the man, according to various sources. The injuries Mr. Shedd sustained in these accidents lead to the decision to surrender his driver's license. "He had a definite aversion to the machine, is what he called it," said one close friend.

It was in one such collision that Mr. Shedd lost his front teeth. In later years, he accrued a collection of teeth, his own being the first of many. His friends saw this collection as a conciliation of his antipathy toward cars in general, and admired the breadth and variety of the collection. "You'd never really know how small a rabbit's front teeth are until Shedd show up with a pair of them, recently taken and scrubbed clean," said Gerome Mainder, the host of the Matinee, the local tavern which Shedd frequented.

Charles Ely Shedd was born on March 12, 1918 in Graysville, Tennessee. He spent his childhood here, with six brothers and sisters. He graduated from Sam Davis High School in 1937. Five years later, he fought in the 45th Infantry Division in Sicily and later in northern Italy.

Upon his return to the area after his service in the war, Mr. Shedd met his wife Jane Florin, whose father owned a carpet company. After Charles and Jane married, Charles went to work for his father-in-law, performing multiple duties, from manning the cash register in the retail floor and installing carpets in homes. "He would never leave a job unfinished," remembered one co-worker. On several occasions, Mr. Shedd would remain in a customer's home long past normal working hours. "The only way to get him to stop before he was finished installing a carpet," remembers one long-time customer, "was to offer him a place at the supper table."

In the autumn of 1972, however, an accident rendered Mr. Shedd unfit for employment. A load of broadlooms toppled over, injuring Shedd's lower back. "Took hours for us to get him free of it," remembered a co-worker present during the accident, "but the whole time, there he was, caught underneath that loom, smiling his toothless grin."

In the last years of his life, Charles Shedd took up reliable residence at the local tavern. His friendship was enjoyed by many of the patrons. One night a fight broke out in the barroom. "Chuck was real kind to the one young fellow, got him a napkin for his mouth, bleeding pretty bad," remembers Gerome Mainder, "even picked up his teeth for him off the barroom floor. Human teeth were his favorite."

Charles Shedd is survived by his wife, Jane, a daughter, and four siblings presently residing in Knoxville.

The old men in Lory's garage sat around drinking their beer and smoking their cigarettes. There was the scent of mildew hanging in the air, of sawdust clumped on the oil stains of the smooth cement floor. It was cold against my bare feet. I was sitting back near the shadows, facing them all, with my back to the empty husk of the body of the car that had been propped up on cinder blocks. The single light suspended from the ceiling swayed in the breeze that would enter the garage through the wide-open front door. The old men faced the dark front yard but did not seem to see it.

I watched the smoke from the cigarettes they clutched between their fingers rise and shift in the light before vanishing altogether against the ceiling of the garage. Occasionally, the smoke they exhaled would stay low and float in my direction and would be drawn up into the shadows behind me and disperse somewhere near the lurking body of the disassembled car. I was idly following with my eyes one of these trails of smoke when I heard a distinct sound behind me.

It was the sound of water being disturbed on its surface. It sounded at once distant and nearby, and I was afraid to turn around. But then I heard it again, distinct in my ears, but attended with the slightest echo. I looked up to see if any of the old men—Shedd and Lory and the others—had heard it, but their rhythmic drinking remained undisturbed, their gaunt faces registering nothing, not even the thin trickle of music from the little radio. I stood up from my chair, with my eyes steadily on them, but with my ears attentive to the sound of water coming from the shadowy recesses behind me. When I heard it again, I turned. There was nothing there but what had always been there, the body of the car, its base layer gray showing faint and dull in the electric light, a battered tin bucket half filled with sand, nails, bolts, copper piping on the stained floor, discarded beer cans, the ornate labels emblazoned on their crushed surfaces hidden in the shadows. I listened for the sound of water, taking a few steps back toward the dark area of the garage. Then I heard it again, unmistakably now, a splash, not frantic, but large, as though something heavy had stirred the surface of an expansive body of water.

I braved a couple more steps into the darkness, away from the electric light that had imprinted itself more faintly now upon the contours of the car there and upon the smooth cement floor cold to the touch against the bottom of my bare feet. The floor of the garage was littered with beer cans, and though I could not see them, I could feel them with my feet as I kicked them to the side. The thought came to me that these cans had not been consumed in lighted parts of the garage then thrown into the shadows, but that they had been swallowed down in the darkest corners of the garage, which were still invisible to me from here.

I tried to think of the sound beer makes when it splashes up against the inner walls of its aluminum container, and I listened more closely, to try to decode it. When I heard it again, I continued further back into the shadows, moving around the rear bumper of the car. Then I was walking full stride, kicking the cans with my bare feet out in front of me and to either side, to clear my path, and they noisily clanked against the cement floor, but the sound that had drawn me there persisted, acquiring a clarity that gave me an indication of its general point of origin. As it drew me back into the darkness, I focused my attention on it, and sensed that it was the sound of water moving over a body, a human body, I knew, because the commotion was deliberate, repetitive, though not frantic.

I could make out the faint outlines of the clutter against the wall of the garage, the tools hanging from hooks and nails projecting out from the shelving framed by two-by-fours, the canisters of old dry-wall mud, of varnish, paint, an old gas can whose craned nozzle reminded me of the gas pump Reggie used to fill our cars each next morning, but as I walked further back into the far reaches of the garage, these objects became less distinct, and my imagination had to fill them in. Soon, whatever definition the small amount of light had lent them was gone. I reached out my hand and felt nothing in front of me. I turned around to find the light, to get my bearings, but saw nothing, then turned again, still unsure of the orientation of my body, then again and again, but was with each turn confronted with the same darkness on all sides, which did not even now need the light to define it as shadow.

There was the sound of water again. I took a couple of more steps in its direction. The only thing I could sense was the cold cement against my bare feet. I followed the sound still further.

Then against my feet I felt something colder than the floor, more beer cans, only these were not empty. They had the weight of the full twelve ounces in them, and they were standing upright. I knelt to feel for them in the dark. They were unopened, slick with sweat on the outside, cold to the touch, and bound by their thin plastic rings. I drew them up together all at once from off the floor. Then out of the darkness there was a voice—still, clear, and very close. It was the voice of Nathaniel. Take one, he said, but toss the rest over to me.

I woke the next morning, and after washing out the taste of beer, cigarette smoke, sleep, and motion from my mouth, we were at Lory's again, in the garage, drinking with the old men, drinking with themselves, each his own portion down.

John was saying that all fighting is singing, an absolute parallel in which one vocal mode swallows up the others, so that the bloody lip, mauling fists, quickened heartbeat, cannot be ascribed with any reliable degree of certainty to one or the other, each bruised into existence by the convulsions of the same foundational undergirdings, and that the great thirst that fuels them both also follows in the wake of both, which is their sheer automotive integrity, knowing as we do that notes fall as bodies fall, and that the ground will suck up either without discrimination, suck it up in awe, what cannot be said in song cannot be said in even the most brilliant blow and counterblow, for harmony in song, Evenene, is a tangling of bodies that only a brawl can hope to approximate, as one tumbles along in love with the other, in a splintered and fitful embrace of the jenny suck and awe, astonishing us out of our being, rescuing its participants out of the dull look of just having been driven off the lot.

He was addressing me, but gazing out into the driveway, and beyond the driveway to the road that had brought us here. The old men were listening, too, but his voice to them must have been coming from far off, or somewhere else, because they seemed drawn inward by it.

I finished my beer and walked over to the cooler to take another. As I was leaning down, the wall of the garage lit up before me. It was the unmistakable beam of headlights, sweeping from one side to the other. Instantly, the whole garage was flooded with light from the driveway.

I turned and saw figures stepping out of a pickup truck and heard the slamming of car doors. There was the sound of footsteps on pavement, and a rush of voices. It was his congregation, and now they were inside. They knocked Old Man Lory to the ground, and his chair went skidding across the floor with the clamor of discarded beer cans. They had John on the ground now, and more came, blocking for split seconds at a time the beams of the headlights as they advanced.

Then the mass of bodies was in the driveway. They had him down in front of the pickup, and I could see their silhouetted arms pummeling him, legs kicking. They muttered their strange unintelligible mantras, in rhythm with the beating. But out of this profusion of sound, I heard peals of laughter, stopped short by another fist, another kick, then starting again, separating as a spark does from the fury of the flame.

This laughter I recognized belonged to John. It was the same shrill fevered sound that had burst out of him when on the road, or at night as he paced before the fire, and it now shook off its guttural aspect and took on the character of a melody, something constant and clarion, at deliberate intervals, in complete accord with the percussive counterparts realized by fists and boots on his body. I struggled to my feet, and over the debris of their entanglement in the garage. By the time I made it outside, I saw them hoisting him into the back of the truck.

They would be driving in search of the mountain, I knew. I stood on the road, catching my breath, after having chased the truck for a ways, staring now at its red taillights growing smaller and smaller in the distance before disappearing as it rounded a corner.

The mountain lay in that direction. It was a huge hulking dark mass darker than the wheeling starry sky above. It was the void that the stars could not swim into. As lovers of the sun, the congregants could not commit themselves to it. Certainly his congregation would never find it, despite its immensity. It would recede from their approach to keep its distance against the miles and miles they would try to devour on the highway, just as it had refused its terrestrial decree to remain low.

It was the same road John and I barreled down after witnessing the full onset of night from our clearing on the hill overlooking the Matinee, the dusk, as he said, being no transition to night, but a transformation in which whatever has already implicitly belonged to night surges to the surface of the things all around us, from their collective deceitful visage enforced by daylight, to the truth of twilight. That transformation was from the forlorn sediment of the diurnal twisting submission to the grotesque sunshining parody, to the symmetry of night, where everything lost its character as an individual thing and joined together at the point of its blood-root, casting off its definition so that it could reveal itself in its ultimate unknowability.

The eyes are bits of fire borrowed from the sun and as a result are sympathetic to its deceptions. The animals and the drunks are the only ones that are not deceived, because they are pure eye and nothing else, pure sense, as we become pure sense up around eighty miles an hour.

He would say this kind of thing while we drank down the whiskey and tried to catch sight of the change that was coming over the valley at dusk. When it had completed itself, we would pack up the whiskey and make our way back to the car, to drive the night again into its full being, together with the Firebird asserting the impossibility of going any further into things. It was also the impossibility of making distance what it could never be but what the whole of the damned race was convinced it must be, John said, otherwise, Evenene, what other meaning could those who slave away each day, toiling with abstractions that harrow the face, and lay the body low, what else could explain it than the lie that an hour of one urgent young night can be split at its beautiful reckless chords and splayed open, measured, clocked and checked.

I now looked back at Lory's house, at the garage light, at the old men sitting as they always sat, clutching their fluid parts, parts of themselves estranged from themselves, bottled by companies in industrial towns up north, but soon to be reunited in the mouth, throat, guts.

The kids driving that truck, I knew, were making the same calculations, trying to translate distance into a force that would draw them nearer to the mountain, and maybe to the other side of it, where life was arranged to those simple equations, not, as John said, out of cowardice or deceit, but because there was no other way to do it, because the engine that shapes the night into an infinite thing can do so only once its machine parts have been delivered up to the shadowy manufacture of this valley, itself the unity of the river we wake to, and the mountain we can never wake to, for it is the drunk's dream of water that individuates them both as it spills from the mouth of its source, and refuses to rest in one place, insisting on its own movement even against the rigidity of the granite facts that shield the composite falsehoods at the core of the mountain. To approach the mountain was therefore to approach the river. To be suspended in the aftereffects of both as they fought for ground, and I wondered if John had understood this all along, and if the fight in him was meant to ease his thirst as he lay vanquished in the bed of the pickup truck plowing forward through the night.

Antistrophic Choral Interlude: Sermon on the Long Black Limousine

We know why the limousine shimmers blackly in the afternoon light, as we know the heaviness gathering at the corner of our eyes. But what has caused it to stretch itself—blister and supplication—in such thanatomantic luxury? What has caused it to prolong the moment of the ritual, where the life that was contained by the shell of the body for that short time has been displaced and acquired by the body of the automobile, the carrier in which the corpse now chants its own requiem for another short time, during this interim of transition from a place of preparation of death to the place of final rest?

There's the long black limousine, and we know but cannot always say with precision why it must settle like sediment into the fluvia of the imagination, signaling the stark abdication that leaves the corpse a hiding place with nothing more to hide, even if we understand why the coffin within the automobile is the encasement of that loss, and the sheen of our own reflection, which we see as mourners the moment the long black limousine passes by, why it is the residuum of the spark that had once inflamed the revolt against the spurs of death.

Anyone mourning, anyone gathered there on the sidewalk of our small town of Graysville, becomes a mourner upon whom the black limousine confers its image of startled surcessation, stinging death, thorny, black, carrying its vainglorious burden, as we are compelled to carry our own burden, this tent, this tabernacle of stunted growth, of life cut short, and it reminds us of a listener who has become at once accomplice and victim in the crimes for which there is no perpetrator save the black veneer we see doubled in the night sky as upon the cold cruising vehicle that bears the body along.

In the sanctified mission of the long black limousine to carry what cannot be carried, to move what cannot be moved, to vindicate life from the first charge of death, which is a sudden and inexplicable immobility spread throughout the body—in this mission we hear news of our own inclination to fall in step with sleep. But are we prepared to restore the animate being to the image we see in the cold, black veneer of the car as it passes, or do we waver in the face of the premonition that closes rapturous around the eyes, at the corner of the eyes, where the salt of the ocean emerges as our own creation, if tears can be said to be our single, harsh moment of cosmogenic deification?

The car stretches forward, extending its reach in through the eyes. And the body stalls there, pausing, idling, for mourning requires as much as the absence of motion as it does the absence of color, refusing as it does to yield to the prosaic demands of life, just as little as it yields to good food, steady paychecks, or any other of life's pleasures. But it must be black as the last night on earth is black; black as the first night after the day of judgment is black; black as the impenetrable void that envelops the moon is black, but we will only understand its slow slow progress once we discern in the secret heart of its engine the brilliant and cosmic display that lures our lunatic gaze to corner us for the kill.

And like any image from which we demand a lasting impression, the long black limousine must carry with it a story:

> The papers told of how you lost your life,
> of the party and the fatal crash that night,
> the race on the highway, the curve nobody seen;
> now you're riding in that long black limousine.

We know why the limousine is long, since it has only a short time to be on display, only one moment in which we may witness its passing, as it is still tied to the body that it carries, for the corpse would decay rapidly in the open air. But are we also aware that it stands in our imagination as the singular prodigal secret of decay, wrapped up in first a dress, then a coffin, then in the trunk of the long black limousine, whispering in song the secret that intones against whatever grains of propriety to which we might be tempted to conform—a bodily curse against the frailness of the body itself carried forward by the engine of this automobile forging through the demands of death, parsing them out from the demands of life?

We might not know why the limousine must prolong its course. But do we know why it is also deaf, deaf because the ears are the only residual life-possession that the dead retain, even after the moment of expiration, even after we mutter quietly to ourselves a farewell that has been gathered up like dead leaves in the heart, and wished against the scattering winds of time, each leaf too frail to demand its own burial, each vein in each leaf the partition between the deaf-mute ears of the reaping undulations of countryside and fireside, where whoever speaks—minister, friends, family, lovers—must speak in tones that have also departed from the prosaic exchanges that fill the ears of birds—our most damning witnesses—since there's something about the voice that cannot be right, that cannot give audience to what the song of the long black limousine articulates in its wake?

The answer, friend, is that as we watch the long black limousine pass by, we are not watching the deceased in that grim pageant. About the deceased there is no longer any question. No question about the deceased, and for this reason it can remain shrouded. The passing, just as the funeral procession passes, is what our attention contemplates in the image of the long black limousine, and our gathering here, furthermore, along the sidewalk, ourselves a long black line luxuriating in the deepest of realizations, is an acknowledgment of our own participation—that we are complicit in finitude, complicit in mortality, because each one, one by one, dear friends, shall one day pass, just as the long black limousine passes.

When I woke the next morning I walked down to the river on the mud and grass path, my bare feet against the cold dew, and knelt, cupped my hands and brought the water up to my mouth, taking it in, and drinking it down. Then I walked back up the path to camp and saw the pickup truck parked there, not far from the smoldering embers in the pit. I stepped quietly over their sleeping bodies, two together, sometimes three, laid out on the ground, covered by blankets, sleeping bags, jackets, arms outstretched, some kept closely to the body for warmth against the early morning chill.

I approached the truck and found John there in the hard-metal bed. His eyes were closed, and his body propped up against the wheel well. I put my foot on the rear bumper and climbed up over the tailgate. The sun was not yet fully up, but in the early morning light I could see his face. His eyes were swollen almost shut, his lips caked with dried blood. A thick streak of blood had hardened in his hair, too, near the ears, and flecks of it still clung to the side of his face. As the sun climbed up over the horizon, now the great variety of shades of purple branching out from gashes and bruises on his forehead and under his eyes became visible. Then he opened his eyes and looked at me, and said nothing.

I heard behind me the sound of bodies rustling in the blankets, the slow struggle of their waking. When I turned around one of them was already standing at the opposite side of the bed of the truck. He yawned, then looked down and opened a beer, bringing his eyes up to us as he tipped his head back and guzzled it down. He smoothed his dark hair back, took another drink, then a pull from a cigarette. From the bed of the truck I watched the others rise from their sleep, stand, look around camp for water, coffee, booze, boots, jackets, car keys. One of them crouched before the pit of ash and dug for flame.

Once everyone had been roused, they started loading up in their cars, some lowering their heads, and stepping into the back seats, others piling into another truck bed, arms outstretched through the open windows, checking themselves in rearview and side mirrors. Then the keys turned, one by one, spark plugs sparked to life the engines, and the engines turned, each with its own unique voice, until the whole campsite was full of their varied and idle roar.

One of the bulkier members of the congregation took the driver seat of the truck John and I were in. He reached over and shoved open the passenger door, and two girls got in, sliding over on the bench seats before slamming the door. When we started moving, John closed his eyes.

I looked out at the valley as we passed through it once again, the motionless trees, the tall grass of the roadside ditch, and on the other side of the treeline the river, which the highway followed for a few miles before breaking off in the direction of the mountain to the east of us. There had only ever been one route, as the next morning became late morning, noon afternoon, dusk night, and this was the route we took now. We did not stop at the Gas-n-Go, but instead passed it by. I watched the sign appear, then saw Reggie on his stool, not looking off into the distance, taking no notice of us as he sipped his RC Cola. Then it gradually moved out of sight as we took a bend in the highway and continued on.

Out in front of us I could see the other cars, all speeding along at the same pace. As we drove on the tree lines opened up to grassy fields that stretched off into the distance, where I could see hills crowned with a single far-off tree, fence lines, woods, before the road again was enclosed by another tree line, whose branches would reach out over the road high above and wall us in. Then, up ahead, I recognized the sign for the Matinee, but it, too, passed by, along with the squat building surrounded by the gravel parking lot and the few cars that rested in it.

The abrupt shifts from early morning to mid-morning, mid-morning to afternoon, and from afternoon to dusk kept pace with our progress, but were now fractured because we had not made the normal stops, had not lingered, as we normally did, in our hazy activities, John's talk, the drink, the music, the tangle of the trees. And so it was dusk again now when we passed the Matinee. As I turned to watch it disappear, I caught a glimpse of the sun suspended just above the horizon, between the clouds, which took all its colors into themselves but reflected only muted shades back.

All traces of the sunlight were gone by the time we passed Lory's. I saw first the opening of the garage from the road, then the single light bulb suspended from the ceiling, and the old men, their postures as they sat in their chairs recognizable even in silhouette. It was visible for what seemed a long time after we'd passed it before it was swallowed up in the dark. I looked at the road behind us, the pavement we had passed over, illuminated by the red taillights, whose reach was meager, though enough to give the yellow lines a violet hue, like veins in the hands, and the red light casting the faintest glow over the dark trees that canopied the road.

I imagined how our thundering down the highway in this absolute darkness would have looked from some distant vantage point, a speeding red pulse breaking through the overhanging branches, alternatively white, red, both at once. In open country, seen from far enough away, there would have been hardly any indication that we were moving at all. This distant perspective, I knew, belonged to the mountain. Its sharp granite inner eye would see us coming, and would never let us get around it.

The procession of cars drove further and further into the night and drove the night further and further into itself. I no longer thought about the mountain to the east of us—its dark presence was no different than that which surrounded us, and so I laid my body out in the bed of the truck, and felt for John there. He was warm, and I could feel him tensing himself up against the crisp night, and against the pain that must have been coursing through him as the truck moved down the road.

I looked up into the night sky, starless and possessing nothing the eyes might cling to to orient the body. I closed them, and opened them again, and there was no difference between what I saw sprawling above me and its convergence within me. I did not try to turn to look at John, but only felt him there with my hand, his body with my body, moving or not moving, at that same pace, present now according to the very same silent ratio, which was nothing like the one of miles per hour that he had clung to as the key to the perverse secret of this valley and our place in it. It was that ratio that decoded the curse that lay wrapped up inside him anyway. I thought of the road at night, the two of us enveloped in the Firebird's mania, as it propelled us forward demanding that we ourselves flood our thirst and adopt the engine's own fury in the face of all peace, stillness, sanctuary, and respite. Only the engine could have discovered this—because, as John said once, it, too, was forced to live, breathe, and slumber imprisoned within the body of the car underhood.

Strophic Choral Interlude: The Suck and Awe

Many colloquial expressions in this part of Tennessee are colorful, comedic, and poignant. There are few, however, as paradoxical as the "suck and awe," which, to my knowledge, is entirely unique to the basin of the Hiwassee River and the localities surrounding it.

The suck and awe of it might be the lightning-storm demise of an enormous oak tree not fallen completely but uprooted just enough to cause its upper regions, its thick limbs and massive dead-cell trunk, to smash into the rooftop of a nearby house. The tar shingles, the plywood underneath them, the two-by-fours comprising the frame—these become disjointed and exposed after the impact. It is a moment of action not frozen in time—I hate that expression and resist its cold-heart indifference to continuity and accuracy, as time is warm like a young woman's breast is warm and hospitable, too; who among us here having felt an hour slip away without a word could recognize anything frigid about time, that hour having accepted the solace of our lazing eyes, our silent tongue, and spiritual appetites without a word of complaint?—so not frozen but caught, motion held in mid-stream, mid-descent, mid-destruction. The suck and awe resides there as a living entity—like a word or a child—in the object itself, which we no longer see as two discrete entities, tree and rooftop, but as a single act bespeaking a natural impetus.

But what is the suck and awe? Is it in the nails rent from that which they had once held together, poking out now, some bent in the act of tearing away, others surviving this act with integrity? Perhaps it is the wood itself. Maybe it is one additional ingredient to the sawdust that comprises the particle board, or the limbs having broken but, in that breaking, having also found a kind of repose such that they can now prepare for the warm disintegrating hand of time to flatten the bright gash-wounds of their exposed cellulosic interior. Maybe it is in the abandoned swallow nest, itself an accretion of the tree's small broken rewards, or the dead leaves on the ground, sinking annually deeper and deeper and eventually comprising the ground, becoming soil and food rot. Whatever it may be, we can be sure of this: the suck and awe has presented itself as an image that merely awaits a voice to initiate its full revelation.

I am not going to make any pretense about knowing why it remains hidden, or by what means. I'm going to instead tell you about the man whose house this tree has destructively complicated. His name is Lory.

When Lory could no longer make it up the mountain, he hung up his rifle and hunting vest and took up a seat at the local tavern, which we sometimes call the Theater but whose actual name, the Matinee, is much more specific and fitting. Local consensus informs us that it got its name from the well-known fact that it is invariably full by noon and whatever shows its patrons are going to put on are in full swing by then. At its deep mahogany bar sit a number of characters, no more and no less interesting than any you might find in such a bar, in such a town in such an area as southeastern Tennessee. Lory drinks beer at this bar, and drinks it well. He has perfected his slouch, his grin, his dexterous handling of a wallet brimming with singles, his overall deportment maintaining a resistance to overstatement.

At night, when the bar gets full of too many people, he moves on to his home or the home of some of his family. He's got two kids who live in the same part of town and one who lives just ten miles out off Highway 27. These kids are equally acquainted with the haggard face of Lory pushing himself through the screen door or opening the offspring's refrigerator to search for another beer, the just rewards—at least in his mind—of bestowing upon these people the gift of life. He has an aversion to the interiors of his kids' houses and in all weather but the coldest he finds himself a wood block or a lawn chair in the backyard. At his son John's house, if his way finds him there, the two will linger in the garage, where an old Firebird sits propped up on cinder blocks as it receives the automotively attuned surgical attention of the young John Stone. The assistantship of Lory is much valued by the younger counterpart, but is of little practical import. Both men know this and neither is bothered much by it.

Lory always makes it home however, by various means, the most common being walking. He rarely looks up at the tree that's smashed apart his rooftop, as it has only above-ground implications. And Lory, for better or for worse, is one who spends most of his time in the basement.

In his basement is a boat he's been making. The inspiration for this effort has, to my knowledge, never seen the light of day. Nor, of course, has the boat. The bark is ostensibly a sailboat, though it lacks yet a mast. The hull and body have been pieced together from various sources of scrap wood, scavenged from nearby construction sites. Perhaps it was there that Lory first conceived of the idea. It is easy to imagine him homeward bound in mid-stumble, stopping perhaps to relieve himself, looking upon all the unused wood—quarter sheets of plywood, two-by-sixes and so forth—and thinking to himself not about a boat or any other useful end toward which this wood might contribute but thinking, simply, that good lumber should not go to waste and, zipping up his pants, stepping over the plastic orange barrier that designated this site as a place of construction, hauling it all home.

Who knows for how long that wood sat without articulated purpose down there in his basement. Was it before the lightning had brought his home the nearby oak? Was that collision of wood on wood the impetus that delivered him the idea of a boat? Boats in general have myriad uses here. One may lose or take virginities on boats. One may drink on boats. One may boat an escape. From boats, cops drag for bodies in the river. One fishes from a boat. Some even bow hunt deer from boats.

But Lory is a man with the ocean on his mind. Distance has no bearing upon the situation, just as it can make no meaningful claim on his decision to walk home from the Matinee in midshow, and just as, before that, had no bearing upon his decision to quit walking up the mountain. And so he proceeds with construction despite the distance of more than a thousand miles that separates him from the nearest ocean. But that's still not the suck and awe of it.

Nor is the moment of contact or despair, the point of departure, the shriek of the canary nor the purr of the cat, the sullen face of one hundred years ago, the shadows that cross the face, the seed that breaks open underneath the ground, the fearless ascent of that seed, sprouting like a river's birth. Nor is the suck and awe of it constituted by the shadows that cross the lawn and the face, the trials and tribulations sung about on Sunday morning, the geological stamp of the river, the nullifying void that grows out of the head of the mountains like a good idea, the best he's ever had maybe, or the second-best to hanging up the rifle. Nor is the suck and awe the Sunday morning calm, the placid faces of those exiting Riverside Chapel, the urge to sink or swim, a hangover to outrun, the sweat that gathers on the walls of the basement, a shovel in possession of ancient clumps of dirt, a rusted maul, the sound of water moving through copper pipes, the flannel couch hospitable to a body too drunk to make it back up the stairs. Nor is it the subterranean view that shows us Lory hunched over the hull of his sailboat, chisel in one hand, feeling for his beer with the other. To his right, a trash can long buried underneath a plumage of Budweiser cans, some of which survived the emptying without then being crushed in the hand or under heel, I'm told. Nor is it the twelve-pack buried underneath a haphazard pyramid of cans, this twelve-pack having been bought, its buyer having passed out in his jeans on the flannel couch down there in the basement, and subsequently forgotten, buried alive one might be tempted to say, but retaining its potential force of something immortal, a spiritual survivor, a living artifact waiting to be unearthed, and someday it might be, someday when the work is going well, when the chisel in hand is moving across the wood surface of the hull, and the thirst quickens the spirit, but the body and sweaty hands desire to continue, perhaps, since memories never die but are only covered by heap upon heap of empirical experiences, maybe since the beer's stayed cold down there in its subterranean storage place, the two will meet again, surface in the old man's mind, and he'll take the few necessary steps, past the old stand-up lamp and grandfather clock, neither of which work, and plunge his hand down into that mass, feeling his way for a live one, find in the weight and inner splash the indelible signs of stored and intoxicating vitality there, and like yanking up a stringer full of crappie, he'll pull up those remaining few survivors, crack them open and return to work.

He calls it work, but of course it's not work. Nor is it pleasure. No, it inhabits his body as a secretion of the mind, fueled by the mysteries of old age—who knows. Maybe it is some misplaced concept of freedom, a concept which must, for Lory, always contain as both necessary or sufficient condition the wide-open eye of the ocean, a thousand meaningless miles away.

One night John and I went down to visit the old man. I could smell the caulking glue he'd been applying to a joint for the rudder. The cat—black in theory but a midnight blue in appearance—was watching him from a corner, yawning, his open mouth looking like an alluring other world wrestled and named, his tail a spike that receded further back into the shadows. Neither Lory nor the cat broke their concentration when John and I entered. John set the twelve-pack down on some boards spiked with old rusted number nine nails. We sat and drank and watched the old man work. The more closely I regarded him, the more I realized that I'd been wrong. He was not concentrating at all. His motions (he was grinding down some rebar, a section about two feet long) were automatic. I sat and thought about the rebar's contribution to the whole but could not guess where it might end up on the boat, what purpose it might serve, attributing this to my own general lack of knowledge of sailboats. His rhythmic movement as he worked to grind down the rebar resembled the very same movement at oar. The metal-contra-metal sound effected by the grinding was soothing. I leaned over and asked John what he thought about the rebar, but he didn't know either. We sipped at our beer, and no one spoke. It was just the sound of that metal moving against the spiraling ridges of the rebar.

John had this story he'd tell. I heard several versions, on several different occasions, but they were all more or less the same. I don't know if it was true, but it sounded true enough. After his mother had died, his old man Lory, for a period of about six months or so, exerted all his energies to taking care of the three kids. He would cook for them what he could, beans and potatoes, corn chowder, and other rustic concoctions. A lot of stews. He'd shoot a squirrel or rabbit and add those, sometimes buy ground beef, tried to maintain the garden out in the backyard, which grew tomatoes and carrots, but failed to sustain it in the end, "due, of course, to unfamiliarity with the habits of the vegetal world," as I heard John put it once. John and his brother Mark were in high school and could for the most part take care of themselves. It was Jane, the young daughter, who'd relied upon the motherly perspicacity the most and who suffered the most when that supply of care ceased. Old Man Lory, for about six months, tried as hard as he could. Money was tight, as it always was, and summer ending. He was intent upon preparing his daughter for school, had entertained the hope that she would not miss a day due to the loss of her mother. He bought her new shoes, the appropriate school supplies, made sure the stew survived the older boys' adolescent voracity by running them out of the kitchen, made sure the girl brushed her teeth and combed her hair. The latter she had to do herself, as Lory had never touched a brush and did not intend on doing so now that he was a widower. He would watch the girl at the sink to verify that she'd worked away at cleaning her teeth long enough. And she was faithful in her brushing, until the supply of toothpaste had started to dry up. Lory cursed her, told her to use less, but it was no use. The girl amassed what were to Lory enormous globules of the rather expensive substance there on the bristly end of the brush. And eventually it was gone.

Now here is where the different versions of the story diverge. I've heard John tell it one way to some people, and another way to others. In some versions, Lory is as pissed as an old coppermouth snake, while in others he's just trying to look out for his girl, make sure her teeth are clean. Anyway it was around that time, the start of school just a few days away, that Lory had taken on some work with a contractor friend of his, Riley, who needed a hand with a drywall job at a house up Highway 27. Lory worked a few days hanging drywall, and after it had all been hammered up, time came for the mud to be applied to the seams. Now Lory had been eyeing those tubs full of thick white mortar, stirring it with an old piece of beechwood, slopping it up onto his joint knife, spreading it and smoothing it over the seams with deft strokes of the hand, and it's not clear when or how he came upon the idea, but one night, he arrived back home with a little jar full of the stuff and set it by the bathroom sink. The next morning, while frying up some eggs, which he'd hydrate with a few splashes of beer—this was the small detail that he thought defined his culinary expertise—he told the girl to go brush her teeth. She obeyed, of course, and, at least this is how John tells it, she was rather enthusiastic about the new supply. She dipped her brush into it, the joint putty, and though a little dry, it re-assumed the consistency of toothpaste when it had been in her mouth. She spit and rinsed and returned to the kitchen table to eat her eggs.

John would always end it there, and I'd never asked him what happened. But I did ask him once if the old man had been satisfied by the revenge he'd gotten on the girl for using too much toothpaste, or if she learned her lesson and so forth. But John looked at me baffled. "What do you mean? He just didn't know any better." I could hardly take this as truth, and it was John's nature to do all he could to leave things unresolved, and the more absurd and unbelievable then all the better. "Hell," he'd added, "she still uses the stuff." This was John's way, too, this slapstick conclusion, his way of spiting his audience's need for conclusions, "for only the weak," he has often said on other occasions, "or only rich folks need their gifts *wrapped*," the general thrust of which I took to indicate that the world presents itself unwrapped, unbounded, and some of us—maybe only a few of us—can take it that way, sucking it down with the rest of the world's awful aporias.

I thought over all of this as I sat down in the basement watching Old Man Lory grinding down the rebar. Added to the rhythm of the back-and-forth scrape was the occasional pop and subsequent hiss of another can of beer being opened. I don't know for how long Lory worked on the thing, don't know how many other sections of rebar he had hiding somewhere among the rubble of his basement. Eventually, I leaned over to ask John what it was for. John finished sucking down his beer, cleared his throat and said, "Hey, old man, what part of the boat's that there for?"

Lory stopped what he was doing. "This?" he asked, holding the section of rebar up for contemplation. "Hell if I know."

The sensitive souls among us will now be in a position to understand the suck and awe of it. But those less confident in intuition, perhaps, will find themselves tempted to ask Old Man Lory just how, when it comes time to sail away, he plans on getting that boat up the stairs and out of the basement.

Five

FLUMEN OUROBOROS

When I woke next it was still night. I heard their voices, mangled before even crossing the gates of their mouths. I opened my eyes and realized we were still in the bed of the pickup truck. I saw light dancing, and raised myself to look around at the camp. In the firelight, I saw a couple of the kids walking around to the back of the truck. They surrounded us and stared.

One of them threw open the tailgate and climbed in. He took John by the ankles and shifted his weight, then hauled him up out of the truck bed. John thrashed around, kicking at the arms of his assailant, but his breathing remained steady, even as he muttered a few curses before trailing off. Then I heard him gasp as he thudded against the ground.

They kicked him a few times, to orient him in the direction they wanted him to go. He struggled up off the ground onto his hands and knees with his head down. He was coughing and spitting into the grass. In the firelight I could see strings of dark blood mingled with his spit and hanging from his bottom lip. They pushed him further away from the truck, some keeping their distance, others moving in to take a shot at him. They prodded him further to the edges of the camp, in the direction of the path I take when I wake the next morning.

I jumped out of the truck and followed them in my bare feet down the mud path. The moon had come out, and I could see them standing around John, lying on the bank. The river itself was beautiful. The surface of the water reflected the moonlight, animating it with the rhythms of its slow movement, the minuscule quivering of the surface, where a submerged rock had interrupted the current, held a quality of light slightly different in intensity than those that surrounded it, so that the water was not simply returning the single reflection back to its single source but was returning to the night sky a whole chorus of lunar presentations, complicating each one, distorting and cursing that single source its singularity, and the loneliness of any solitary existence. And then I drew my eyes further up across the river, up to the bank and the far side. Standing there on the far bank was Nathaniel. He was watching us.

Without removing his shirt or shoes, he approached the water, taking the first step, steadily and decisively, then another step further into the river, unflinching as the water moved up to his waist, then shoulders. He simply walked into it, his body fixed upright, showing no signs of the influence of the current. The water submerged him, glimmering where he had went under for a moment, before it was restored to its original dark grain.

Soon, his head reappeared, then his shoulders, chest, and he was still walking with his fixed pace toward our side of the river. Then he was standing among us. He looked at all the congregation gathered before John, and looked into their youth, dirty hair, dirty hands, filthy necks, at their clothes tattered by nights spent out here in the open air, in the grass and mud. He regarded their cigarettes, the bottles and cans they held. He looked them all in the face, one by one, the way I had seen John looking at them in the face, when he would implore them to drink and curse the day downhill. Nathaniel passed his eyes over each one, slowly, and when they fell on John, lying in the dirt, he walked over to where he lay and crouched beside the corpse.

He reached over and ran his hands over John, feeling the outside of his denim pockets, then turning his body over onto his other side, feeling the other pocket, moved in closer, and reached into it, pulling out the money, the few bills and coins, that would appear the next morning when I'd wake. Nathaniel stood and pocketed the money. Then he knelt and sidled up next to John, thrust his arms at the waist, and heaved the body over his own broad shoulders.

John Lee Stone, Aspiring Local Musical Talent, Is Dead at 19

John Stone, a teenage wastrel with a propensity for violence, was found dead on the banks of the Hiwassee River early Monday morning. The cause of death was fatal loss of blood from multiple stab wounds. He was 19 years old...

The head of John Stone, a local high school dropout who enjoyed drinking and fighting, was found wrapped in a blanket in the back seat of his Firebird early Monday morning. The decapitation was, apparently, executed with his own buck knife...

The body of John Stone, a cowardly and garrulous tough-talking son of a bitch, was found covered in urine, bruised, beaten, sodomized, and outraged out in the woods near the Hiwassee River early Monday morning. The cause of death was blunt trauma to the head, apparently by an empty glass bottle...

The soul of John Stone, a teenager who unjustly attacked wanderers in the night, was condemned to the bottom of the Hiwassee River early Monday morning, after Stone was strangled to death on the muddy banks...

But you cannot count on death to count the composition or start the process of decomposition if the voice of the dead is still echoing throughout the valleys. The flash of lightning which steers all things cannot know what it truly demands until the clap of thunder that it sends out in all directions at once has reached the ears of all creation, before disintegrating upon the horizon as a whisper that carries with it only the slightest hint of its secret of divinity, come down from the clouds, connecting the invisible circuits that confute the schemes of mankind by which he maintains the separation of earth and sky.

And you cannot count on death to know the fabric that it tears in two. The alternating lights which stream from the tops of ambulances and squad cars can only repeat in alternating rotations the resurgence of the night in the pools of blood that seep down through the surface of the highway. And you cannot ask of death to recall the beauty of the earth adorned in her youthful garments. For it was death itself to whom she sang in her early days to keep her body beautiful.

Nathaniel carried John down the bank, downstream, on a path that I had never noticed before. I followed him down it, stopping when he stopped to put down the body and catch his breath. And I walked on when he heaved the burden back over his shoulders and continued lumbering down the path. I could hear his labored breathing as he walked, his mild cursing between breaths, his sighing as he stepped over a deadfall in the path, or over a stone that had split it.

We walked for a long time. The moon seemed further off now, less bright than it had before. The river had narrowed, the surface of it more complicated now, but the water itself dull, gray, showing nothing of its glassy grain, but only hues to match the sky, as it tumbled through the valley, over rocks, over the smooth gliding bodies of the catfish, past riverweeds, whose stalks trembled in the current.

Then we came to a point where a smaller stream converged with the river. The ground was soft there, and I could feel my bare feet sinking into it. The path wound through a thick patch of cattails, their bulbous tops suspended in the air, balanced on stalks that seemed too thin to hold them up, as they leaned and shook against one another in the breeze. I could hear on my left the little creek, paralleling the path that hugged the edge of the main river, the Hiwassee, which I caught glimpses of through the underbrush, for the sun was almost up, and the world again was in the process of being restored its definitive character, the rigid outlines of its component parts, each asserting itself against the other, with the belief that it would be able to maintain its material integrity for the momentary flash in which the sun describes its arc across the sky.

I stopped when I realized I could no longer hear the labored breathing, or the steady pace of the man I had been following. The only sound was of the water, flowing into itself here, and of the cattails rustling in the breeze, and I knew I was lost.

There was a story John told me once about a young girl who woke early one morning and set off for the river in search of the famous coppermouth snake. They cannot be found in swift waters, someone had told her, and so she sought out a low marshy runoff a few miles away from here, where the weeds swept from side to side up above her head, so that when she looked up all she could see was open sky. Her step was light. She had only a blanket or nightgown wrapped around her shoulders. She wore no shoes, and the water came up over her ankles. She moved slowly, lifting her foot out of the water, a thin stream of it trickling down the bridge of her foot as she suspended it there for just a second above the surface, before swinging it around in front of her to complete the next step. Her eyes scanned the lilies out in front of her, resting for a moment on those points where the cattail stems doubled with their own reflection and emerge up out of the water. It was early in the morning, and the voices of insects were beginning to flare up around her. The breeze, which usually begins in the morning, moved the heavy heads of the weeds above her. She slipped in between them, lifting first one foot up out of the water, then planting it in front of her to complete the step. She never took her eyes off the vegetation before her.

Now the coppermouth exists first as a dark brown or black spot just above the surface of the still waters. It is indistinguishable from the vegetation and may look like a dark wet stone floating impossibly among the lilies. But when you get closer, it will become an open flower of iridescent bronze flecked with cyan and pearly white, slicked and fanged, though the fangs are hard to see because they are nearly translucent. They are, instead, John said, only implied.

Her bare feet would pause at the bottom before settling into the mud or rock. She would feel the stems of weeds, clumps of submerged root, or the strange give of a stick covered in mud at the bottom. You never see the mouth actually open. One moment you're looking up ahead at a motionless tableau of marsh. You'll take your eyes off it for just a second, then looking again you'll see it there, the flashing flower of the poisonous open mouth. It will vibrate in the field of vision, and it will make you cringe with recognition. The little girl froze, her foot suspended above the water. A few inches? A few feet? Who knows how close is too close. But she could have held this pose forever. She pulled her foot away, and the serpent's mouth, detecting the motion of an intruder, opened further.

In this story, at least the way I've heard John tell it, we are reminded that the coppermouth drinks only rainwater. The old-timers used to know when it was going to rain because they'd see these serpents mythopoetically dancing with one another on front lawns or off the shoulder of the highway, slithering up against one another in an ancient and graceless sway, their shimmering mouths opening toward heaven, waiting for the first drop of water, even though they live their entire lives in water. These creatures have been known to follow a thunderstorm a hundred miles.

Once things dry up, they make the long trip back to the river, a perilous journey considering the chicken hawk and falcon, the pickup trucks and young kids with their .22 rifles, and their sworn enemy of course is the Firebird, which swoops down after the long interval of death, for that great bird loves to use the serpent to wipe away its tears of ash after rising from its coeval sleep and loves, too, to fuel its inner combustible machinery with the poison of the coppermouth.

In some versions, the girl gets the snake by the tail, for he who is all tail can only be gotten by the tail is what John says. She has with her a pillowcase and uses this to capture the snake. She lunges at the brilliant head of the creature, and with the open end of the linen traps it for the necessary moment—for a moment is all she has—before swinging it up out of the water. Inside, the snake's muscular body snaps wildly back and forth, and she rushes out of the marsh and onto dry ground. She holds the pillowcase away from her body and returns home.

She goes into the garage with her captured quarry, sets the pillowcase on the work table. On the edge of the table is a vice grip, which she proceeds to crank open. With a hoe, she forces the snake's head into the vice grip and clamps it in. Its body moves in the air as though it is trying to swim, yet there is nothing frantic about this movement: it is patient, methodical, and full of spite. The girl rummages through the tools on the shelf and finds a pair of needle-nose pliers. She forces the mouth open. She tests the grip of the vice, and once certain of its secure hold on the creature, she begins to pry first one of the fangs then the other out of the coppermouth.

Once both fangs have been removed, she forces the snake back into the pillowcase and takes it into the bedroom she shares with her brothers. Spots of blood, mingled with the snake's venom, darken on the bottom of the white linen case. She tosses it onto the floor of her bedroom, jumps up onto her bed, and waits for the creature to find its way out of the opening.

Epodic Choral Interlude: On the Origins of the Hiwassee River

Imagine with me a lone wanderer, accompanied only by the sound of his own footfall, the crunch of the dead leaves beneath him, the cry of the chicken hawk. It is a commonplace belief among solitary woodsman that each being in the woods has its own voice: the black walnut tree's voice emerges from the vibrations of its soaring leaves as they are disturbed by a leaping squirrel. We are all familiar with the sound that follows from there. But we may be less aware of how this sound compares to the human voice.

Down there in the throat, man's own bodily breeze ascends, the air undergoes changes effected by the physiological mechanism at work, the vocal chords, and comes out as something intelligible to those around him, or to himself if he is alone. From those effusions we impart sentience to the being who manipulated the air in such a way that it could be recognized as a voice and from which could be inferred the presence of a mind. But we attribute no such sentience to the trees. Is that because we have not yet recognized a pattern, a language, have not yet sorted out the distinctions a tree might want to make, distinctions upon which its very life might depend? Or is it because we deem accidental the arrangement of the leaves and the air that moves through them? Who is to say the thoughts that arise in the solitary wandering woodsman do not belong to the living members of the greater environs, the trees and birds and the microbes, which disrupt the air with their tiny circumambient vibrations and which can be detected in times of what we, in our less discerning frames of mind, might call silence?

Now it has become a commonplace attitude of woodsmen to assert that the various organisms found in nature have a voice, that they speak to the man with the ears to hear, just as they make their presences known to the wanderer with the eyes to see, maybe the nose to smell, the thirst to drink in such images, sounds, and bodies. I have no inclination to counter such claims, nor to naively endorse them. Rather, these claims regarding the sentience of natural phenomena shall presently serve as a point of entry for the discussion of the origins of the Hiwassee River, which is the occasion for the following remarks.

Stories regarding our Hiwassee proliferate here. What distinguishes our river from other rivers across the nation and elsewhere is the sheer number and variety of these stories. You cannot pass an evening at the Matinee without hearing about how the riverbed was laid in the distant past as a secret escape route for the spirits inhabiting the mountains to the east of here, and how when those spirits were caught and slain by our local heroes, their blood formed the first fluvia of the Hiwassee. Likewise, a person could live his whole life here in this town and one night, perhaps at dawn when the liquor starts to settle in and the great gray owl has gotten his fill, hear a story about the origin of the Hiwassee that had never been heard before and shall never be heard again, or maybe when getting gas at the fill station hear about how Hiwassee waters were the liquid remnants of some great mythopoetic canary's song which grew too heavy and sad to remain in the air. And so forth and so on.

Some stories of the origin of the Hiwassee mingle Biblical tales with local lore. I once knew a Presbyterian who enjoyed telling about how in these United States, and particularly in this part of Tennessee, the men and women before Noah's flood were so sinful that the Jehovah Jireh did not even need to send down rain to drown them, that all he had to do was sweeten the waters flowing down from the mountains, and these gluttonous folks promptly gorged themselves on it, their bellies burst open, and they all subsequently drowned.

Another, more interesting story borrows its originating device from the very same jawbone of the mule with which Samson in the book of Judges had slain a whole battalion of

Philistines. According to this apocryphal tale, his strength was so great that he was able to throw the bone all the way from the Promised Land, across the wide open mouth of the Atlantic Ocean, and land it right here in our backyard. A spring emerged from the bone, or so this particular story goes, and that spring became the source of the Hiwassee. The tellers of this tale have the benefit of not only explaining the appearance of the river but also of at once asserting the strength and accuracy of the great Old Testament slayer.

These portmanteau tales are common enough here and can be heard on any number of diverse occasions, in reference to the unique genius of a local high school quarterback's arm, for instance, or in a conversation with the local butcher, and during times of intense spring rains.

Perhaps the most interesting account of the origin of the Hiwassee, however, is one that I have never since heard repeated, neither in a bar nor in a church. The story is a variation on the well-known report we have of a fascinating Cherokee tradition. The Cherokee, when it comes time for him to die, walks out into the woods and sings a song which has never been sung before, a song which he has been composing his entire life, but which has remained only in his mind, its melody, lyric, and cadence unknown until the decision has been made to leave this world behind. Now when the first European settlers of the area arrived here, they brought with them, among other tools, weapons, and sicknesses, a unique kind of written language which we call musical notation. It was one gray and perhaps stormy afternoon when an old Cherokee warrior recognized that it was his time to walk out into the woods, sing his death song and lay himself down to die. A white settler, while deer hunting nearby, heard this song and did not know what to make of it. Having had some musical training, he pulled out his feather-tip pen and transcribed in musical notation the Indian's death chant onto a pad of stretched beaver skin. The old warrior, once he had finished singing his last song, sat down on the forest floor and waited for his last breath. Meanwhile, the settler, after shooting a sizable buck, returned to his mountain home, his wife and children. He was fascinated by the song and showed it to his wife. The whole family started singing it, found it a beautiful creation, blessed praise to the deity they had brought over the Atlantic with them. Each morning, upon waking, they would pick up their crudely strung instruments and sing the song. Little did they know that each time the song was sung, a Cherokee would, as though under some kind of spell, wander out into the woods and die. The Indian camp suffered greatly, as each morning another member of the tribe would wander out into the woods and lay down and find there upon the ground a last bitter breath. They would all go to the same place, drawn to the same deathbed, perhaps since the song was the same, and this bed eventually filled with corpses in various stages of disintegration and the ultimate fluidity of its fate, which had gathered and become a formidable force moving westward, through the woods and linden groves, through the meadows and savannas, until joining the Tennessee River about fifty miles away. Thus the river came to be known as the Hiwassee, derived from the Cherokee name "Ayuhwasi," which means meadow or savanna.

This is just a story of course, filled with the anachronism and callousness toward its subject common to all stories. But we permit a story its incivilities and suspend our judgment because of the pleasure only a story can offer us. It doesn't ask to be believed, only heard, and for that we're grateful.

Another story, which I want to conclude with, holds that the Hiwassee was formed from the guts of the infamous serpent himself. In this version, God has just created the world, but not yet the human race, and no garden to corral them, nor fruit to tempt them. The serpent and the Lord are, then, on good terms more or less, which is essential for the thrust of the tale. The story goes that the serpent wanted to make a contribution to the creation and approached God with a proposal to build a river. God walked around the face of the earth in his rawhide boots and Stetson, surveying the land. He decided that it would be geologically expedient for there to be a river coming down from the Appalachians to the west, something to contribute mountain spring water to the Tennessee River. He delegated the task to the serpent, who enthusiastically donned his engineer's hat and set to work. After a few delays and the passage of a considerable amount of time, much to the relief of the great tempter, the project was completed. The serpent, who wasn't very bright, invited the good Lord to come inspect the work. But what God saw bored him immensely. There were countless problems with the project: the water was too muddy to sustain wildlife, there was nothing to protect the land from flooding, the trees were not sufficiently varied to supply the ground its necessary nutrients, and much more besides. God was upset with the serpent, to say the least, and he removed his hat, as he always did when there was some serious thinking to be done. He looked the serpent over, and instructed him to lie down on his belly and stretch himself out to receive his due punishment. His tail was touching the Appalachian mountain springs, and he was told to stretch his body out and drink of the Tennessee River. Then God Almighty raised his boot heel above the head of the serpent as it sipped at the serene river water, and kicked downward with swift and celestial force, crushing the creature's head. The good Lord took out his buck knife and slit the belly of the serpent open. The guts spilled out, and soon the muddy intestinal banks hardened, forming physical barriers in the landscape. Vegetation took root along the banks. The mess of the snake's innards eventually gathered a current and cleaned itself of its gore, sediment, and sanguine parting, life emerging through the gradual but sure-fire processes of nature. The fish found it suitable to their needs and animals arrived to feast upon the fish. God considered his work and as he cleaned off the blade of the buck knife on his blue jeans, he called the thing the Hiwassee, and exulted in its force and beauty.

It wasn't that the coppermouth couldn't be found in swift waters, though this was true enough and she knew it. What they really told her was that there was an important part of the story the Book of Genesis leaves out regarding the serpent's punishment. This was that God took away the evil snake's ability to speak by first injecting him with poison then filling his mouth with delicate fangs.

Once the girl had heard this, she crept through the muddy wash of the slow part of the river in search of the coppermouth. She held her pillowcase ready. She suspended her foot above water, slowing her steps as she surveyed the marsh before her. She set her bare foot down, and it sank in the rich sediment under water, then lifted the other up out of it, the submerged earth clinging between her toes. A rivulet of water ran down the bridge of her foot as she held it there for a moment, before slowly submerging it once again to take the next step forward.

And there it was: the iridescent bronze blossom vibrating in the field of vision. She opened the mouth of the pillowcase and ever so slightly approached the snake, whose own mouth had opened also, and maybe she heard a hissing sound, though this would be impossible, John says, since the snake makes no sound, no voice left, just poison and fangs, as a part of his punishment.

She captured the creature. It snapped at her, but the thin linen barrier was sufficient to keep her safe. The snake whipped its body back and forth against the fabric that had imprisoned it. She leapt out of the water back onto dry ground and headed home. She entered the garage, secretly, and heaved up the pillowcase onto the work table. With her skinny little arms she cranked open the vice grip. Once open, she picked up a nearby broken rake and used the sharp end to force the head of the snake into the vice grip. With her other hand, she cranked it shut upon the head of the snake. Once it was secured, she wrestled free the fangs from the flesh with a pair of needle-nose pliers. The snake had stopped moving, save the small vindictive thrust of the tail. With the splintered end of the rake, she forced the coppermouth back into the pillowcase. She took it into her room, jumped up onto her bed and waited for the creature to find the opening.

Jennifer Evenene, Beloved Daughter, Dies at Age Thirteen

Jennifer Evenene, the youngest daughter of Mr. Lorraine Evenene, was found dead in the marshy shallows of a runoff of the Hiwassee River early Monday morning.

The cause of death has yet to be determined. The local police suspect drowning, though they are not ruling out the possibility of other causes.

A local boy found the body while walking along the banks to go fishing. The boy was alerted by the sight of the young girl's white nightgown. "Looked out of place," said the boy, whose identity shall remain anonymous for reasons of privacy. The boy dropped his fishing pole, ran home and told his eldest brother about what he had found. Police arrived a half hour later and had the body escorted to the coroner.

Born in the autumn of 1964, Jennifer Evenene lived a brief but happy life with her brothers and father. Local church members enjoyed the sight of the bright-faced girl on Sunday mornings, and will remember Jennifer Evenene's brilliant Easter dress. "She will be missed," said her father.

A memorial service will be held at First Presbyterian on Highway 27 at 1:00 PM this Wednesday afternoon. The funeral is scheduled for the next morning.

When she arrived back home, she slung the pillowcase up onto the work table. She cranked the vice grip open, this time with a force that she had never before felt in her arms. Her bare feet were still wet.

At her feet, she saw the handle of a broken rake. With the sharp, splintered end of the rake, she guided the head of the coppermouth into the vice grip. She threw it down and cranked the grip to hold the head of the creature. With a pair of needle-nose pliers she worked the translucent fangs from the shining mouth.

When both had been removed, she took a nearby knife and slit the belly of the snake. Its guts fell onto the cement floor of the garage. The smacking sound startled her, and she dropped the knife. She then picked up the two fangs, placed them carefully on her tongue, tilted back her head and swallowed them down.

ACKNOWLEDGMENTS

I want to thank my friend and editor Tim Kinsella for all the hard work he put in getting this book in print, Celeste Carballo and Cassandra Jenkins for designing the book cover and for always supporting my work with blessed faith and lovely voices. I would like to thank those friends of mine who have encouraged my creative endeavors—Mat Petronelli, Jessica Milton, Peter Bradley, Devin King, Karl Levy, Ami Xherro, Alexa Winstanley, Dirtbike Dave Pemberton, and Mary Magdalene Serra. I'd like also to thank Nick Pappas, from whom I learned about the virtues of grace and decency, and Waylon Jennings, who has been with me through these years of lonesome city life. And finally, for their commitment to all that is good, I'd like to thank my mom and pop, my sister and my brother.

ABOUT THE AUTHOR

Keegan Jennings Goodman was born under the sign of the Virgin, grew up in the Ozark Mountains, lived for a while out on the west coast in California, went to college in Harlem, then art school in Chicago, and now he lives in Toronto where he is writing a dissertation on the French philosopher Georges Bataille. He enjoys hunting, fishing and the company of his friends.